TO BURN IN RAPTURE

R.A. RAINE

Book Cover by Getcovers

Illustration by Emily @the_megabee33

Editing by Brittany at BLD Editing

Ebook 978-1-7638024-4-5

Paperback 978-1-7638024-5-2

Special Edition Illustration Cover 978-1-7638024-6-9

1st edition

To all the lovers who have the odds stacked against them
but choose to burn anyway.

R.A. Raine

To all the women who never gave up.

Sabine

To my cor animae meae. You are my eternal rapture.

Janus

Author Note

This story spans a time period of nearly 3,000 years from 752 BC to 2025 AD. All time periods are noted at the beginning of each chapter. In no way do you have to understand ancient history to enjoy this book. It is ultimately a love story based heavily on fantasy.
And if you are a history buff, in no way is this story historically accurate.
Happy reading!

To Burn in Rapture uses Australian English.

Content Warnings

Before moving forward with this story, please take into consideration that this romantasy does contain darker themes. In these pages, you'll find an FMC who has lost touch with her humanity and a god who cares for no one but her. You'll also find child loss to be a recurring topic. Please only read on if you feel prepared for the subjects fully listed below.

War; Child loss; Grief; Blood; Murder; Pregnancy and birth (in the past, descriptive); Descriptive sexual scenes; Physical abuse; Sexual assault (in the past, not detailed); Graphic language; Mental health themes.

The Roman gods of

To Burn in Rapture

Caelus, God of the Sky

Janus, God of Beginnings and Endings

Pluto, God of the Underworld

Prosperina, Goddess of Spring and the Underworld

Latin to English Translations

"Cor animae meae": My soul's heart/heart of my soul

"Me cor laceras, anima mea": You're killing me, heart of my soul

"Mea amor": My love

"Cor meum, pausa": Heart of my soul, stop

"Vale": Farewell/Goodbye

Three songs I listened to on repeat while writing this story:

1. "Ma Meilleure Ennemie" by Stromae and Pomme

2. "Ruin My Life" by Zara Larsson

3. "Ordinary" by Alex Warren

The Legend

It is told that Janus, Roman God of Beginnings and Endings, broke one of the godly commandments: thou shalt never feed thy godly blood to a human. In an act of rapture, Janus gave a drop of his blood to a dying woman. Upon seeing her soul, he was brought to his knees, unable to let her go.

This is their story.

She's Mine

The Past, 752BC

A uburn hair fans out around a delicate face—a face bruised and bloodied. My natural inclination is to move to the next soul, to keep pushing through, opening door after door, but she stops me. A slightly sweet rose mingled with blood and ash fills my senses. Her almost lifeless form pushes at the men around her—men who are ravaging her body in undeniably brutal and carnal ways.

War plays around us. Soldiers dressed in blood-stained tunics overpower all manner of women and girls, but it's not them who hold me in place, who draw my body closer.

The need to make myself visible to her grows vaster and deeper by the moment.

I have no care for where I am on this mortal plane, but I know innately that I'm in a Roman village. A place I'm sure was once filled with the bustle of market stalls and children's laughter. Now, all I see is chaos.

Fire burns thatched roofs, and hordes of burly human men capture women to take as slaves.

Before, I thought it was the human way to be so barbaric towards one another, but as I see this woman before me whimpering small gasps of "No," her cheeks washed with tears, I find it hard to step away.

Maybe I can help her? The thought comes unbidden, a scowl working its way over my lips as I step before her prone body on the dirt below.

Her blue-green gaze meets mine, not quite turquoise but an amalgamation of the two colours, drawing me in as she whispers, "Help me."

That's when I realise I've dropped my barrier. The ward I keep in place—that all gods keep in place so humans cannot detect us when we are within their realm carrying out our godly duties. Once we make ourselves known to a human, there is no going back; the invisibility magic is lost to them, and they forever have sight over the god who dropped their shield before them.

Millennia ago, we used to let the humans see us, worship us, but they grew obsessive and destructive on a whole other scale. In the end, we all came to the decision they would only know about us through myth.

But here I am, showing all seven feet of my body to a dying human because she's as good as secured a one-way ticket to the Underworld, and I can't let her go. Not to him. Pluto can't have this one.

She is mine.

Where did that come from?

Something thumps in my chest, my gaze ricocheting back and forth from her eyes to her captors. A strange feeling bubbles within my stomach at the sight of her being pinned down.

"Who are you?" a gruff man from beside me grounds out.

They can see me too. My guard must be fully down for my shield to casually drop before this group of humans. And now that he's seen me, he has to die. And by the look of the other soldiers' lingering gazes on my form, they also see me.

They will all die.

My thumping chest grows louder in the cavities of my eardrums, making me wince.

How do I soothe this ache?

I want to thump back at the pounding in my sternum, but that will do nothing. I have to save her. I know that's the only way this erratic feeling will go away.

Turns out this human is gaining her wish.

I will help her.

It won't come without its own set of complications, but for once in my monotonous existence, I will take something for myself.

She will be mine.

The Past, 723 BC

She can't see me yet, but I see her.

Her body is resplendent in a simple cotton night dress, sitting in an open field next to a silver-haired woman whose heart no longer beats—not like my cor animae meae, the woman I saved with a drop of my blood. She brought my soul's heart back to life, and she will forever be its keeper.

Tears stream down her face as she gazes at the older lady. The urge to go to her and dry her face instead of hiding behind the tree line nudges at my legs.

My heart kicks up in pace—a strange feeling I haven't gotten over since the first time I saw her.

Our eyes clash.

Seeing the beauty in her features makes me want to fall to my knees in my toga, but I have a job to do. I cannot stay here and gaze upon a human all night.

That would be wrong.

I may have called her mine, but we can never be.

We are doomed to linger in the periphery of each other's lives.

She begins to stand, her lips poised to spill words I must not hear, so I leave.

The Past, 678 BC

She's my new obsession.

I have to stay away, but my body physically cannot. I keep being drawn to her over and over, and I think she realises death is an easy way to find me. As soon as I smell her intoxicating, sweetly human scent, I stop and watch her until she inevitably notices me, unable to draw myself away.

Now, she's busy trying to plaster a wound while unaware the body she is working on is already gone. Seeing her care and compassion for the humans has brought out a sense of humanity that was missing in me before. I wouldn't go as far as to say I care about them, but I show more interest in their affairs now. Maybe they are more than just barbarians. And just maybe, they know something about the heart we gods haven't quite figured out yet.

I wonder if she will talk to me again today.

Her green and blue eyes flick up to find mine. An exasperated gasp leaves her lips as she lets the people around her know the boy is gone.

Once they disperse, she comes to me.

"Tell me of your heart?" I ask the woman who has stolen mine, and she regales me with stories far beyond my imagination.

The Past, 520 BC

Her eyes find mine, and it's as if I'm falling down a never-ending galaxy where only she and I exist.

I love so much about this creature—my human.

I don't know if I can hold back from her much longer.

There's an ache I feel in my body for only her.

Fates, what have I done?

If I don't consume her, she will consume me.

What a Wimp

Present Day, 1st June, 2025 AD

G *ods, have mercy on my eternally tormented soul.*
Humans are so fucking dumb. Another day, another mindless sheep trying to sell me the latest and very
much overpriced handbag. I stare closely at the stitching
on the quilted black clutch, an obnoxious C plastered in
the middle. The stitching is atrocious, and the leather ... I
roll my eyes, and the sales assistant hustles out of sight. I
don't even know how they can slap $10,000 on this piece
of crap.

"Not the one, baby?" A hand slinks around my fitted black minidress, pressing me into a solid frame.

My frown turns into a smile as I spin within my husband's firm grip, my long blonde hair falling over my shoulders. "No, baby," I sigh, running my fingers up a broad-chested torso covered in a smooth black tee. "I'm bored of this place. Can we go home?"

I'm bored of this life, this fucking existence. The fire in my stomach roils and deflects. *Him.* I want to see *him* again. It's been—gods, it's been maybe eighty years since I saw him on those bloodthirsty battlefields back in 1944. This happens every time I start to feel this way. My hands itch to feel bronzed skin under my fingertips again, but instead, they find fair, creamy skin like my own.

Four days' worth of stubble lines Grayson's cheeks. He doesn't like stubble or beards. He thinks they make him look unkempt, not like the prim, spoilt, upper-class rich boy he's used to being. It's taken me a solid five years to work him into more casual attire. He's got a sexy body with a lean, muscular figure, strong jawline and piercing blue eyes. He just never knew how to use them to his advantage until I showed up.

I push my toes into my crisp white sneakers so I can climb my fingers up his chest and around his neck. "Come on, baby." I kiss his stubbly jawline, a spicy musk hitting my senses, my body shivering at the contact. I've taught him a few things I'm eager for him to distract me with when we get home. "I need you inside me."

"Fuck, baby, you can't say things like that in public," he says in a hushed whisper, bending his head towards my ear. We are still working on dirty talk in public. When we met, Grayson Hawthorn the Third was a fourth-year Oxford student on the cusp of walking into the family business, a multi-billion dollar finance company. He'd had one long-term girlfriend since his first year at Oxford—Lou something. She was old news pretty quickly when he laid eyes on me, the older, mysterious Oxford postgrad with a penchant for running into him frequently on campus.

One exceptional—*if I do say so myself*—blowjob later, he dropped Lou like a bag of rocks and moved me into his London penthouse. Daddy Hawthorn had bought it for him as a graduation present.

Pushing my body flush against his, I let out a moan just so he knows what I can feel growing inside his pants. "Fuck," Grayson says under his breath, hauling me out of the store. Looking back, I find the two store assistants gaping at our hasty retreat. I give them a solid wink. Grayson the Third might be a posh prick, but he's a sexy posh prick, thanks to me.

A black SUV idles by the sidewalk for us, and Grayson offers me his hand as the driver opens the door. I scoot towards the end of the back seat, my husband following at a distance. When he gets desperate like this, he can't bear to touch me. It's like he tries to forget, but he can never forget me. None of them can. I make sure of it. I've given Grayson everything he has ever wanted in a partner. I play the modest housewife for his parents and business associates, and when it's just us, I give him mind-blowing sex and the leader he secretly craves. One thing I've learnt in my nearly 3,000 years here on earth is that men are all the same. As long as you have a pussy and are willing to use it, they will give you whatever you want.

You just have to choose your targets wisely. I don't always go for rich and pathetic. One time, I married a kind Scottish farmer who'd lost his wife and baby to the labour of childbirth. He had this cute cottage overlooking the ocean in the countryside. We kept all sorts of animals, and for a time, I thought it would be enough—maybe kindness was the cure—until my skin started to crawl, my blood started to boil and my heart screamed for a man I couldn't have. It always ended that way. Grief would take me, sucking me down deep into its despair where all I could think of was him. The one man I could never have.

Lost in my thoughts, it takes us a few short minutes before we are at the ostentatious building that houses the penthouse. This time, the driver opens the door, and I follow a swiftly moving Grayson as he sets foot in the glass entryway to the building's lobby.

"Come on, Sabine," he almost whines as he stands at our private elevator, eyes impatient with lust.

"I'm coming," I murmur under my breath, my legs carrying me hastily towards my husband. When the elevator doors close behind us, he's on me, his body pinning me against the wall, fingers digging into my hips.

"Do you feel what you do to me, Sabine? You fucking drive me crazy. Four fucking years, we've been married, and I still can't see or think of you without getting a hard-on." *Awww, I love it when he waxes all poetic for me.*

I roll my eyes, facing the wall. *Fucking idiot.* Luckily, this elevator is devoid of mirrors, and he can't see the scowl ruining my features. He was fun for a few years—sometimes still is—but it's all getting so repetitive. He's just like the rest. He could never match up to *him*.

Grrr. Fuck. Don't think of him. Shaking my head, fingers travel up towards my chest, kneading the soft flesh. No bra, of course, because that was the worst invention since the pill. Watching this world turn to shit in a handbasket over the last 2,798 years has been a fun ride, but one I wish I could bypass.

Fingers pull my pointed nipples, and just for drama's sake, I push back into the rock-hard cock lined up against my ass, wondering if I'll let myself have fun tonight.

"You like that, baby? You like it when I'm rough with you?" Grayson groans into my hair.

It's the only time I like it. He worked that out pretty fast in the early days. Pain is my pleasure. When you spend an eternity having your heart ripped out of your chest over and over again, how else are you meant to find joy?

I take it through pain.

"Mmm, harder, Gray." He usually stops at making me bleed, but I have no such qualms. I married a fucking weakling. I'm sure *he'd* not approve, but that's the whole point, right?

The elevator door swiftly opens, and Gray swings me bridal-style in his arms. I shriek at the unexpected movement. "You want hard, baby?" A smirk graces his perfect, straight-toothed smile.

"I don't have to beg today?" I ask quizzically, my eyebrows furrowed.

He laughs a deep belly laugh as he strides into our bedroom. "No, baby. Today, I'm hungry, and the only thing that's going to quench my thirst is seeing you on all fours as I pound you into the next century." *Unlikely, but I'll go along for the ride.*

My body is flung onto the bed. I bounce on our super king, black silk sheets fanning around me. "You're not even going to eat me out?"

Grayson removes his T-shirt, followed by his dark blue jeans, a serious hard-on reaching out for me beyond his grey underwear. "Nope."

Fuck yes.

I groan out loud, flopping onto my back. "Is it my birthday or something?" I ask, smiling up at the high, vaulted ceiling.

What can I say? I love it when he fucks me senseless without any prep work first. He usually hates starting that way, complaining about the friction, saying it hurts his precious cock, but I live for the fucking friction.

Told you he is a wimp.

I really tried to make a man out of him instead of some stuck-up douche in a suit, but it's hard to weed out the posh prick when it's ancestral.

A dip in the bed comes first as Grayson climbs towards my feet, naked, his cock standing at attention, already dripping pre-cum. Turning for him onto all fours, I flip up my dress, showing him my ass.

"Fuck, I think that's my favourite thing in the world. Next to your tits, of course, and your lips. Hmmm." His warm fingers run across my skin, little jolts of anticipation shooting right to my clit at the thought of what will happen next. Pulling across the black lace G-string barely covering my lower half, he hums loudly. "No, this is my fucking favourite thing."

I grin wide, turning to look at the glazed-over expression on the man lining up his cock at my entrance. He's not the biggest I've had. Funnily enough, that title goes to the mute farmer in Scotland. Now *he* used to fuck me senseless. Hardly gave me any warning too—would just throw me over his shoulder while I was cooking dinner or weeding the vegetable patch and screw me until my voice was hoarse. That's a man who could make me bleed. Eventually, he got sick, though, and I thought the kindest thing I could do was end him swiftly. The strangest thing was that it was like he expected it. Like he was living every day, just waiting for me to shove a knife into him.

Argh, the good old days. Maybe I need to find myself another farm boy. Or a cowboy. I'm a sucker for a cowboy romance. How does an immortal woman find herself a dirty-talking cowboy who will ride her wilder than a bull?

The thought of sexy cowboys has me licking my lips and moaning loudly just as Grayson shoves his cock into me.

"Fuck, baby, you're so tight." He pulls back out and pushes in again. My mind reels as the friction of us moving together makes tingles run up and down the backs of my thighs and stomach. A hand comes down—*somewhat hard*—over my backside.

"Harder, Grayson." I push back into his body, making his next slap more brutal. "Yesssss," I say as I feel the mark of his handprint still on my arse cheek. His body slaps against mine with every thrust.

At his rough thrusting and slaps, it's not long before my pussy is dripping all over his cock, making him groan out in ecstasy.

His hands move under my G-string, finding my clit and pinching the little ball of needy flesh. "Come on, baby, I want to feel your pussy strangle my cock."

Pulling on me harder, he continues to thrust, our bodies smacking together, making wet, suffocating sounds that only make me needier for release. I grab at the front of my dress and pull it down, revealing my breasts.

"Harder, baby. Please, I'm so close," I beg Gray, crashing myself into him as I pull on my nipples. My whole body feels shockwave after shockwave of sensation through my limbs until he finally gives my clit one last flick, making me fall over the edge.

My husband flops over my body, thrusting one more time before spilling himself inside me, moving his hand up to cradle my stomach. "Maybe this will be the time," he whispers lazily into my ear, his body engulfing mine.

I want to slit his throat at the mention of a baby. It's the one thing he's desperate for. The one thing I cannot—no, *will not*—give him. I had a baby while I was immortal, and it didn't work out. How can you make a person immortal but not her child? It is my one point of contention when it comes to *him*, the god who made me like this.

"Baby, did you hear me? We need to start talking more seriously about getting you pregnant. Mother and Father are asking for grandchildren. Mother keeps asking what you do all day without children to run after." *I can't believe this imbecile is asking me for children again while his cock is still wedged inside me.* I roll to the side, his cock popping out of me. "Oh, come on, baby, you can't get angry about this again. We said after five years, we would start trying."

Pulling my underwear back in place and pushing my breasts back into the top of my dress, I glare at him and laugh. A sort of deranged, sarcastic laugh. A bit wild. *Oh, well. Nothing he hasn't had glimpses of before.*

"It's been four years, not five," I point out.

Grayson rests the back of his head along the custom velvet frame of the bed, arms stretching behind him. *Good to know someone is relaxed after he just got his dick drained.* "Baby, come on, we've been together five years."

Taking a deep breath, I exhale. "We've only been married for four."

Since Janus made me immortal in 752 BC, my menstruation has been like clockwork, my body a temple of health and strength forever stuck at twenty-two. This means every year since I was made immortal, I've experienced a monthly bleed—no exceptions. It's no cakewalk being a woman, but I'd prefer it any day over being a man. Women are the true gods of this mortal plane. We create life, after all.

I don't ovulate for another ten days. When I do, I usually just suck him off or distract him with the back door so there's no surprises. I really should just concede and agree to have his posh babies—it would make my life easier—but having a little contention in our marriage is fun. I like a good fight, but Grayson does not.

"Fine." He puts his hands up like I'm about to shoot him. *Maybe I will.* "We'll table this for three months. But that's it. After three months, we are going to have a proper, sit-down discussion about this."

I want to laugh in his face. That is his solution to everything: board meetings about our marriage. Tilting my head, I squint down at him. "If you think you have a say in what happens to *my* body, you have another thing coming, Grayson." My hands hold firm on my hips as I scowl at him from the end of the bed.

The burnt cinder in his eyes flickers for a second; a moment of fight that immediately goes out again. We both know who wears the pants in this family. "Fucking christ, Sabine, give me something. You're such a bitch sometimes." His hands fold through his now messy brunette hair, grimacing.

My blood boils. *That word. This fucker knows how to push my buttons.* Usually, it's just when he's had a few too many scotches, but today, he must be in a mood. Luckily for him, I'm always in a mood.

"Well, fuck you too, you bastard. I don't even know why I stick around when all you do is whine about babies," I huff loudly, my hands flying into the air as I spin on my heel, heading for the wardrobe.

One ...

Two ...

Three ...

Four ... I count in my head. Waiting.

The mattress springs squeak as Grayson leaps out of bed. Two firm arms come around my waist, pulling me into his naked chest. I shudder at the contact. "Shit, baby, I'm sooo fucking sorry. I shouldn't pressure you.

You're right. I'll table this conversation until next year, I promise."

See? I told you he was a wimp. Can barely handle a fight. Usually, I can only get him riled up when he's been drinking, but he must have been bottling this baby thing up for a while. *Sounds like a* him *problem.* Especially since I plan on laying the flowers on his grave in less than a month.

Beginnings and Endings

Present Day, 7th June, 2025 AD

"That's it, baby. Fuck yes," Grayson hisses as I pull languidly on his cock. I thought I should make it nice for him since it will be his last time.

I took him to his favourite restaurant for dinner before we came back to the penthouse. I even dressed up for him, wearing his favourite red peekaboo dress, black heels and makeup. I'm pretty sure he thinks it's Christmas. As I bop my head rhythmically along the smooth edges of his cock, I wonder if I should aim for the heart or the throat. *He's only this way because of his hideous breeding. I shouldn't punish him for it. He gave me a good-ish life. I've never wanted for anything. When I was with the Scottish farmer, I never wanted for anything either. Just Ja—Shit, don't think about him. You'll see him soon enough.* My heart aches at even the thought of tanned skin and dark, wavy hair. Hair that shimmers like the night sky.

My lips slide off Grayson's cock, and I look at the ground to avoid the turmoil threatening to spill from my eyes. *Get yourself together, Sabine.* Wrapping my hand around his hardness, I pull, hearing a grunt from above. *Don't get all weepy just before you see him.*

When I call on the god, it is always a mixed bag of what I become. Sometimes, I will be gripped by anger, sometimes grief, and other times, unadulterated lust. A couple of times, all we've done is stare at each other, not uttering a word until he kisses me senseless and leaves me shattered all over the floor for the millionth time.

I'm sure it's not the millionth, but it feels like that, especially when you've been alive for as long as I have.

Tugging harshly, I say, "Lay on the bed, Grayson. I want to fuck you."

"Yes, wife," my husband answers as he flies onto the bed, his cock standing to proud attention as I crawl up his naked body. My head finds his thick length, I give it one last leisurely lick before finishing the ascent.

"How bad do you need me, husband?" I ask just for fun. Sometimes, I like to toy with my pets before they die.

"I'm desperate for you, Sabine." His eyes roam my naked body. "You're the best thing that's ever happened to me, baby. Fuck, I love you," he groans out as I sink down onto him.

My lips twitch upwards. I watch his face contort in bliss, my body bouncing up and down on him as he grips my hips, helping me slam down a little bit harder each time, making me moan. *Maybe I should at least let myself come before I send him off. I should get something out of this too.*

Coming down hard, the pulsing in my lower abdomen moves steadily to my core, inching me further and further towards bliss. My pelvis hits his over and over. I run my hands through my long hair—my newly dyed auburn hair, a familiar colour from long ago that brings me to new heights because *I did it for him*. I've tried many different shades over the past hundred years, but knowing it's time to call him back, I want him to see *me* and be reminded of the *us* from centuries ago. When I saw myself in the mirror, it brought me straight back to that youthful girl in Italy, to a time before he saved me. Though, when you are twenty-two forever, it's hard to shake the youthful part. According to my driver's licence, I am nearly twenty-nine.

"Fuck, baby, I'm goin—SHIT, I'm going to cooome." Grayson's cock jolts inside my pussy, and I slam down one more time at my peak, ready to explode. *Fucker nearly deprived me of my own orgasm.*

I pull at the strands of my hair, squeezing my eyes shut. Janus's amber irises shift behind my lids. I continue to imagine a muscular frame and wide, dominating hands. My body shudders over the prospect of knowing he'll be here soon. My nose fills with the scent of crystalline beaches in anticipation—that warm, briny smell.

Until the man underneath me squeezes my arse tight, reminding me of his presence. *Right. You.* His eyes are closed as he basks in the feel of us joined in post-orgasmic bliss. Moving so I lie flat over his front, I kiss along his jawline, reaching my right hand for the knife I placed under the pillow earlier. Silently moving, our bodies still joined, I lean back so I can look down at his face.

His boyish smile finds me, and I give him a soft peck on the lips. "You know, you would've been cuter if you just kept your mouth shut."

Grayson's eyebrows knit together as I bring the sharpened butcher's knife to his throat and slice deeply sideways, making sure to hit all the major arteries. Leaning back, I'm careful to avoid the slight spray of blood oozing from him.

His eyes are wide. He tries to say something. Grayson's mouth opens, but in seconds, his lids flutter closed, and he's out. I don't always aim for the throat—sometimes, it's too messy. Usually, I go for the easiest shot: the heart. There's a poetic sort of justice I find in that organ.

Climbing off my rapidly declining husband, I place the knife on the bedside table and watch as the life leaves his body. Waiting.

I don't even bother cleaning the trickle of cum moving down my legs or the sweat that beads my skin.

I just wait for *him*.

Grayson's hands jerk. Then, nothing—

And I wait, standing next to my dead husband, naked, my heart beating rapidly. My head is a dizzy haze. I don't even know if I can string two words together. *Fuck, what will I say to him? "Nice seeing you again. Yes, that is jizz*

*from the dead guy on the bed leaking down my thigh. Hey,
you want to fuck on his corpse?" Too much?*

CRACK.

That sound is a calling card for my weary, barely beating
heart as I spin to see him standing before me. The air is a
sizzling entity around us.

Janus, the god who immortalised me 2,776 years ago.
The god who took pity on a poor dying girl about to be
raped for the umpteenth time. I still don't know what
the catalyst was that pushed him to make me immortal.
Perhaps a glimpse of love? He once said it was the only way
to keep me alive, that he couldn't bear my pleading. But
I wasn't the only one pleading for help on that summer's
night.

All I remember is a numb body and asking for his help.
He'd looked like an angel.

I don't know what I had left to live for at the time, but
the idea of death terrified me. When I saw that golden,
bronzed creature with the darkest of mahogany hair and
piercing amber eyes, I thought he had come to save me for
sure, that he would be able to bring me back to life. And he
did; he gave me a drop of his blood and told me to forget
him and *never* speak of our interaction with anyone.

He later told me the gods had only two rules. Rules they saw fit to make after showing themselves created more trouble than it was worth.

Rule number one: don't let the humans see you.

Rule number two: don't give humans god blood.

After spending time with Janus's blood working through my system, always keeping me strong and healthy, forever frozen as a twenty-two-year-old, I understood the gods' need to make boundaries. I couldn't imagine what humans would do if they became immortal. Even in their mortality, they sought to destroy. If they were immortal, it would be utter chaos. Hell on Earth, if it wasn't already.

Ultimately, I agreed to keep my immortality a secret, never telling a soul. But I never forgot him.

After decades of my body staying the same and an unfortunate accident where I fell off a ship and should've drowned in the raging seas below, I realised for the first time death would never come for me. I've sought him out ever since, becoming somewhat obsessive.

I pick prey I inevitably kill to open a doorway for my god to enter through. It might seem harsh to kill humans since I am one, but I no longer see life and death through fear anymore. Instead, I see it as a rebirthing into a new existence. And as for the dickwads I choose to marry, they are in need of a helping hand to change. It's not my fault that helping hand comes in the form of entering a new plane of existence.

Janus's bright eyes and perfectly sculpted features give nothing away as he stares at me. He sniffs, his nose slightly in the air, and I notice the minute change of his form. The way his seven-foot frame curves inward the slightest bit, hands fisting.

He can smell Grayson on me. I just know it's killing him. Even if it's only killing him a fraction of the way it kills me to have another man inside me, I know it's enough. My petite body stands strong as Janus takes punishing steps towards me.

Pupils slide from the tips of my toes, following the leaking of my pussy all the way up to my peaked nipples and wide eyes. When he stands one foot from me, I gulp—an involuntary reaction to having a god stand before me. A god I've been in love with for thousands of years. A god who shatters my heart every chance he gets.

Not even glancing towards the dead man beside us, Janus stares me down, death and creation a daily occurrence for him.

Shooting my shot, I take a step towards him, my heart breaking out of my rib cage to beat alongside his. He wears a pure white tunic and beige pants that look expertly cut to his lower half, his tunic low enough to cover the hefty bulge I know he keeps tucked away below.

Before I can reach him, Janus takes a step back, his eyes thinning.

Fine, let the stare down begin. I cross my arms over my naked chest, inadvertently pushing up my breasts. My skin prickles with new sweat at the smell of endless summer sunshine. His irises cleave me in two.

Without warning, my eyes start to mist, and I see his stern facade break. I wish he didn't make me feel this way; my heart tearing in half at the sight of him, knowing I'll never have him beyond this sick way of connecting.

Groaning, he reaches out to cup my left cheek. My heart gallops at the contact, my vision blurring. His warmth fills every inch of me at the smallest of touches. "Sabine," his voice rumbles out, smooth but strong and firm, like a king presiding over armies. "You must stop this."

His words are always the same. I have to be careful. If the other gods know of my immortality, they will hunt me down. *The rules* he will inevitably remind me of. They will imprison me in the Underworld—Pluto's dominion, the god of Hell. And though Janus doesn't mention much of the other gods in my presence, I can sense he has history with this particular god. He is hell-bent on keeping me away from him. But I have no qualms with a fresh change of scenery, so if Pluto is my way out ... maybe I will take it.

Untangling my hands, I reach for his arm, feeling muscles contract under my fingertips, skin almost sizzling at the exchange. A hiss leaves the god's thick, kissable lips. My eyes find his again, and he shakes off my touch. I love knowing I have an effect on him, my heart galloping towards him, my body blazing to its very core.

Stepping into my frame, he takes both sides of my face in his hands. I puddle, a lone tear escaping. He catches it with his thumb mid-flight down my cheek, rubbing the offending offering against my skin.

"Sabine, you need to stop this. One day, it will not be me who walks through that door." His eyes plead with mine.

My voice comes out small as I answer him, my breath somehow finding its way out of my body. "But how will I see you?"

Janus exhales loudly and brings his nose down to mine, our tips barely touching, "You should never see me. Gods are but tales, fiction on the wind. We are not meant for human eyes."

Another tear escapes. I curse my body for breaking like this. "But I want to come with you. Please." I grip his wrists fiercely. He caresses my face with his thumbs, his eyes closing, another deep exhale leaving his body. He doesn't even need to breathe, but he does around me, like my human body aligns him with the natural form of his being.

"Sabine." His voice is harsher, angrier this time as he answers me. "Do not make this harder than it needs to be. You may be immortal, but you are no god, and only gods or the dead can come with me. You know this. I cannot thwart the rules of creation more than I already have by immortalising you."

This time, it's my turn to close my eyes and breathe deeply. A warm nose rubs against mine, more tears moving down my cheeks. A soft kiss falls on my left cheek, and my whole body alights, waking up for the first time in eighty years since he last found me, heart torn and bloody on a battlefield of a war that garnered no merit.

Another soft kiss finds my other cheek before pushing back again.

"Sabine, look at me." I almost abhor the thought. I know he's getting ready to leave, to take Grayson's soul through the door.

"Sabine," his authoritative voice comes out. My eyes ping open, my core leaking for a completely new reason. His nostrils flare wide, a low growl emitting from his upper chest. "You must forget this. Forget me."

Gripping the front of his tunic, my sadness is suddenly replaced with rage, a fire burning at his words. "So you will just leave me in this world to watch the people I love die without ever being able to follow them into the afterlife, without ever being able to follow you? What sort of life do you expect me to live? I'M SICK OF LIVING."

It was all too much around 2,000 years ago when I lost my baby—a life that shouldn't have been a possibility, not when I was immortal. *How can he not see that I've become a shell of myself?* I kill people because I know there's a place waiting for them, that they will reincarnate back into another life. I don't see consequences in life or death anymore. They are all portals, beginnings and endings, and all my beginnings and endings belong to Janus.

"If you do not take me with you this time, I will happily call for Pluto to take me to the Underworld."

His effervescent, bronzed skin turns a shade of red I've only ever witnessed a few times as he grips my throat hard, cutting off my breath. Holding me up, my feet dangle above the carpeted floor. My silly human body struggles for air, but Janus and I both know it doesn't need it. "You will do no such thing, cor animae meae. You will live your life on earth for the both of us, do you hear me? I will not have you throw your soul away for me. Do you hear me, cor animae meae?"

My eyelids droop. I reach my struggling fingers for Janus's head, attempting to weave them through his luscious, soft waves. His grip loosens on my neck, my body going to suck in a deep lungful of air. He pulls me towards him and inhales my scent. "I'm sorry," I croak into the smooth skin of his neck, his veins popping out as I kiss delicately along them. My body vibrates in harmony with our connection, and I bring my legs around Janus's waist. He grips my bottom with his broad grasp, fingers flexing over my heated skin.

We do not speak for a long period as we hold tight, basking in the way our bodies melt inward towards each other, the way our hearts find rhythm in one another's, the way our souls sing deeply. "I've indulged you for too long." The heart-wrenching sentence falls, and my heart breaks. I swear he hears it crack because it's all I can hear as his hands don't make a move to release me from his body. "Live your life, Sabine. Find people who can truly love you back. This can never be," he mumbles the words close to my ear, trying to break my heart. Trying to sever the cord. "Stop waiting for me."

He finally finds the strength to pull my legs away from his hips, and I let him.

"Stop hurting the humans."

He yanks my hands from around his neck and places me on the floor. I stare up at him, unmoving like a sick spell has been cast upon me. One where I have no choices, no way to change this life. No way to make him want me more. My soul bleeds out, my body immobile, dead.

"Leave me be, Sabine. I will not tell you again."

He steps backwards, his lips a hard line as he looks back at me.

"Stop acting like a child. I'm sick of seeing you like this."

His gaze rakes over my naked, cold body.

Slowly closing his eyes, he lifts them to my face again, and this time, his voice lowers an octave. "Don't make this harder for yourself, Sabine. We will never be."

Turning on his heel, a loud *crack* befalls the room. Janus blinks out of existence. No backwards glance. No chance of us.

My knees sink towards the carpeted floor. Noticing how wet my cheeks are, I rub my face, numb within my body, finally locking away my heart to the world and everything beyond.

If Janus won't have me, I'm done with living. I'm done with this life. It's time for option B—or option P.

My God

The Past, 333 BC

I can't do this anymore. I can't watch someone else I love die. Years of this turmoil. Janus only visits when death is on hand. *I hate it.* This time, it's a close friend of mine, Bryn. An illness has struck her down. No one is willing to go near her, too afraid they will catch it too. I—the only soul prepared to stay close by her side—feed her soup and bathe her wounds. I guess immortality is good for something. I've played nursemaid to many a sick patient, mainly for purely selfish reasons.

All I want is to see him again. My god. The one being I would bow before, if only he would give me the chance.

I'm in a small settlement in Celtic territory surrounded by lush forests. The area is ripe for producing native dandelion and rosemary—herbs I use daily in treating any disease that goes through the mortals.

I've been treating Bryn for many moons, but her health has been ever-declining. Seeing the pain on her face only makes it even more apparent that mortals will always go through the full cycle of life. And even though I'm hurt because I'm losing someone dear to me, I'm also envious because I don't think I'll ever have a beginning or ending again. This is it for me. I am forever destined to be the witness.

The war in my mind is nearly as bad as the pain in my heart.

As soon as she passes, he's there in the small, inconsequential room in Bryn's hut with a ringing *crack*. He comes to me full of grace as he wipes my tears from my cheeks.

"What can I do, cor animae meae?"

"Take me with you," I answer as I clench his white robes. He pulls me into a tight hug and eagerly sniffs at my hair.

"Cor animae meae, you smell like spring. Your heart is too good for this place. If I could take you with me, I would. You know this." He pulls me back, earnestness leaking from his amber eyes. "All I can give you is this moment," his deep voice rumbles through his chest, making my body tighten in anticipation of what might come. He doesn't always lie with me. Sometimes, we kiss. Other times, we talk about my life, and he basks in all my stories, telling me I'm living for the both of us. Knowing that helps bring some ease to our separation. He tells me how his existence is an endless loop of life and death. It's not romantic, so we try to stick to my adventures instead.

"I want all of you, then, just for a little while," I say. He almost looks pained, his dark eyebrows gathering together.

Cradling my face in his hands, his gaze softens as if coming to a conclusion. "I can give you some time."

My face burns with an ear-splitting grin. I leap at him, barely able to contain my excitement. Having a friend die should dampen my need for him, yet it does not. Knowing her soul is in my god's capable hands is liberating. I hated knowing she was suffering, and now she is free—a luxury I'll never be afforded.

Lush, thick lips instantly descend on mine, swallowing me whole. My body rapidly falls into his touch and embrace like coming home. My blood sings for him. *Cor animae meae.*

He feasts on my mouth, nibbling on my lips slowly and deliberately, his tongue coming out to play. I fall open for him, our tongues dancing together, each of our strokes sending shockwaves of ecstasy down to my core. *I love this god. I love him with my whole heart and soul.* The thoughts are unbidden. They feel like they are mine *and* his, ours.

I climb his body, finding myself fully wrapped around him, his hard, thick length grinding against my clit, my core dripping, knowing what it wants from Janus, needing what only he can give.

"Please, please, cor animae meae," I plead with him over and over. He grips my hair in a tight grasp, my bottom firmly in the other hand.

"How wet are you for me, cor animae meae?" he asks, though I know he can smell me.

I smile ruefully at him. "Take out that monster between your legs and find out."

A smirk overtakes him, only making his sharp cheekbones and strong jawline even more devastating.

"Me cor laceras, anima mea," he growls closely to my ear, making a shiver rack my body.

Pulling back from him to see his darkening amber eyes, I whisper back, "You too, my soul's heart."

Holding his gaze on mine, Janus moves us to a rug in front of the stone fireplace without missing a beat. Placing me carefully on the thick material, he nuzzles into my hair. "Tonight, you are the god, mea amor."

Raining kisses over my face, neck and chest, he begins to move south, hurriedly ripping and pushing down my simple cotton dress and undergarments as he goes. I moan and writhe underneath him, each kiss sending tiny electric bolts running straight to my pussy as he lingers on certain sensitive parts of my skin, nipping and licking. My hands find his hair, encouraging him to keep going.

Soon, he has the last of my undergarments ripped away. Pushing my knees apart, he growls loudly at the sight of my swollen pink flesh—a claiming. I'm sure if anyone was around, they would get the message: I am his. My body overheats with his lingering stare alone, my pussy dripping on the rug, waiting for him.

In a blink of my human eyes, Janus is now naked before me, using his powers to undress himself as he stares down at me. "Why didn't you do that to my clothes?" I huff. The ripping was hot, but I made those clothes with my own two hands.

"Because I wanted to ravage your body with the appropriate fanfare a goddess deserves." He quirks a brow and moves down between my legs, eyes not leaving my own.

"Oh, oooohhh, oookay," I moan as he dips his tongue between my folds, eyes still trained on my own. I shut my mouth, no longer complaining.

"And now I'm going to worship at the altar of the only body that means anything to me in this godly existence." He licks again and again, eyes still trained on mine like he cannot miss a single second of my reactions. My pussy pulses for him as he takes languorous lick after lick until I'm a sweaty, horny mess underneath him, begging for release.

"Please, Janus, I need you to suck my ..." I try to say where, but his tongue moves in and out of my core, lapping me up.

"There, cor animae meae?" Gods, I nearly come from him calling me that name he uses. That fucking name means everything to me. It tethered us together centuries ago, along with his blood.

"Nooo, up," I whine, and he chuckles. I try to pull his head up. He nips at my swollen flesh, making me cry out.

"Tell me where exactly, Sabine." I tug his hair roughly, which only makes his sweet chuckle turn rumbling. I glower at him.

"Suck my clit, you tease," I ground out in frustration and rage.

"There's my goddess." He wastes no time and heads straight for the promised land. With two short flicks and one hard suck, I'm falling hard.

My eyes flicker out, and I'm slightly aware of tempestuous amber eyes watching me and a heavy leaking from my core. Soon, those eyes are right in front of me, a full pressure pushing at my opening and a sweet kiss on my mouth.

In one hard and swift movement, Janus plunges inside of me, our bodies trembling at the closeness. *Finally,* they whisper. Utter, blissful fullness overtakes me.

"You are my humanity, my family, my sanctuary, my comfort, my joy. I am not sorry for my greed. For taking an angel from the stars. Now, you are my angel, and I will keep you forever," he prays to me, his body encased in mine.

Swiftly, we move together. My legs wrap around his waist, encouraging his thrusts, encouraging his heavy groans of bliss as I match them with my own. *"Love me harder, love me faster, love me forever,"* we both seem to be saying in the only way we know how—through our bodies and words from the old language.

The building in my core grows to new heights as I begin to see stars in the man on top of me. The god cannot keep his eyes off me. We continue to kiss each other until our lips are raw and I'm screaming his name loud enough for the whole settlement to hear.

After he releases his cock inside of me, he allows himself the luxury of lying in my arms for another five minutes before he is up and fully dressed without barely a second thought.

I lie back on the rug, staring at him. He looks beautiful and thoroughly fucked with his hair all tousled, his lips impossibly swollen and his eyes on fire, burning down at me. He looks like a young man, even though we both know he is older than sin.

He runs a hand through his hair. "I don't want to go," he says hastily.

My heart pangs at his words. "Don't. Not today," I say, raising my body onto my elbows. I cannot bear to hear how much he misses me, how much he loves me before he leaves me with his seed leaking from my body. It's not fair. Nothing in this world is fair. I hate it.

He nods his head, eyes beginning to liquefy. I've seen all sorts of emotion in this god in our strange dance between life and death over the years, but this is the first time I've seen him this physically upset by his leaving.

Rapidly, I drive myself towards his body, latching onto him, running a hand over his soft, stern jaw. "What is it?" The need to comfort him is strong.

His whole body shakes as he grasps me tight saying against my ear, "Don't hate me."

I pull back and frown at him. "I think by now, that would be impossible."

"Cor animae meae." He brushes down my hair, giving me a sorrowful smile, a last kiss on the lips, forehead and hand before leaving with a *crack* out of my life and with a new, much-improved dress on my body.

The Bluffs

The Present, 7th-8th June, 2025

After cleaning myself up and collecting my backpack of essentials from my wardrobe, I left, my extra-large hoodie hiding my face from the many security cameras around the building. It won't be long before they find Grayson's body. I planned it that way. Every night after dinner, he calls his parents. *Fuck, I know. He was such a baby.* When he inevitably misses their call, they will send the doorman to check on him. I left the front door open.

It's surprisingly easy to get away with murder. If they don't have any evidence of you and they can't find you, case closed. To the government, I'm invisible. My IDs and passports have always been fake. When you live as long as me, you know how to keep yourself hidden from the outside world. The gods don't know I'm immortal, and now the humans don't know about my existence.

I'm a ghost, forever stuck to haunt the people of Earth.

And to be honest, I feel like killing Grayson was a mercy. Now, maybe he can come back and make something of his life. His parents were keeping him stuck in old patterns and ways of thinking. What I did gave him freedom. When you've been alive for thousands of years, death becomes more of a gateway. You see the soul more than the body. Being trapped in your body is the worst sort of torture, and I've lived with it every day. Grayson was blessed; he got to escape this world. I will never be afforded the same.

Not unless ...

Unless I do the unthinkable: summon Pluto. Make myself known to another god.

I was left numb at Janus's words earlier. Surely, he didn't mean them. He always comes for me. He would never leave me. He is my one constant.

My feet carry me down the empty sidewalk until I find a black cab idling by a corner, a passenger vacating.

Running to catch it, I greet the driver hurriedly and tell him where I want to go. "The bus station, please." *Less cameras that way.*

"Alright, darlin', hop in." We peel away from the curb, street lights flashing past as we weave in and out of London traffic. My hands shake, and my knees bob as the cab speeds along. I clasp them tightly together, aware of the slow rhythm of my heart. Just a *thump... thump... thump* as we drive along, nothing keeping it alive anymore, yet it clings onto life because of that one drop of blood from Janus millennia ago. I don't plan on going far—just far enough to get away from London. In fact, I have the perfect place.

Standing overlooking a Scottish bluff, I'm reminded of simpler times. I kept the cottage from the farmer, Kai. A relic of centuries passed. I couldn't let everything we'd worked for be redeveloped and have all that nature spoilt. I had to forge some documents at the time, but that was a period when people just took things at face value.

This is the only place I feel some connection to in this fucked up world. When I had put the knife to his chest, the old bastard held my hand and pushed, helping me go deeper. I kissed his scruffy, wrinkled cheek as the life left his eyes, and Janus showed up shortly after.

That day, Janus took my hand, called me his cor animae meae and made love to me on the floor of the living room as my husband's soul crossed over. He was tender and sweet. He knew I needed the comfort. It had been at least a hundred years since our last visit. Kai was the first human man who made me stop and think that maybe I wanted more in this life, but he had his own share of heartbreak. He'd lost his voice as a child to a disease that destroyed his vocal cords, and his first wife was his childhood sweetheart who died during labour, along with their baby. We met because I was the only one who knew how to sign within the village. I never sought him out; he just fell into my lap. I was trying to reform myself at the time, hoping I could be better, do better. Stop the killing, stop the need to see Janus. Stop craving him. But it's impossible to stop a drug when it's already working its way through your system.

I saw myself in Kai, and he saw himself in me. I think that's why we got along well. Also, it helped that he could never talk back. We'd sign the important stuff, but most of our relationship was a speaking of souls.

Taking a deep inhale of the salty air, I hear the waves crash below on the choppy cliffs, a familiar dance of mother nature, a knocking on the door. *When will you let me in, Janus?*

I know he said no. I know he said stop, but like I said, he's a drug. His blood is in my blood, and I can't stop wanting him any more than I can stop my heart from beating. I actually think the only way I die is if he dies. But Janus has neither confirmed or denied that statement when I've spoken it aloud before.

Heading back into the stone cottage, I start a fire in the hearth and get to heating some hot cocoa. Eating is not a necessity. I once went decades without drinking or eating, just the sun and moon sustaining me. My body had gone through the pains of hunger, but after a while, a switch flipped and another energy source took over—the god source.

These days, I mostly eat or drink for enjoyment. I love the feel of hot drinks in cool weather, how the warm concoctions slither through your veins like a hug. Plus, you can never have too many sweets. Bakeries are my second drug of choice, next to Janus.

Sitting in Kai's old, wooden rocking chair by the fire, I sip the sweetness of my hot cocoa, savouring my last comfort on Earth.

Tomorrow, I am going to do the very thing Janus forbade me from doing: summon the god of the Underworld.

Amor

The Past, 332 BC

Nine months later—nine *fucking* months later—I lie keening on the floor of a large women's only tent. The space is dressed in candles, feather pillows and furs, the soothing smell of lavender in the air. *Knocked up by a good-for-nothing god. How does one even get pregnant by a god?* When I slept with Janus, I was still seven days from ovulation. Makes sense for him to have super-god sperm since he is immortal. *Note to self: make sure people die at a more appropriate moon cycle. Easier said than done.*

The women around me chant in a circle as my midwife encourages deep, even breaths, her hands pushing on my naked belly. "The baby is coming soon. Can you feel her?"

When the child comes, Janus will. I know it. After he left, I found myself without my monthly bleed, and I just knew. It didn't seem like it could be possible, but I also wasn't aware of many women sleeping with gods. Maybe it was wholly plausible. We had slept together for years on and off, and it was the one time something happened.

His face, those shining amber eyes, knew before he left me, like the timeline had altered in my presence and only after our coming together did he see the consequences of our actions.

Now, I know why he didn't want me to hate him.

"Argh," a cry comes from my lips as another round of thumping pain makes its way along my back.

Moving onto my hands and knees, I feel the midwife touch the head crowning between my legs. "So close now. The baby is almost here," she encourages. Which is a relief because I have been in labour for a whole night and day already. I am ready to be done with birthing. Ready to hold my baby. To hold mine and Janus's child.

Giving one last, guttural breath, my skin dripping in sweat, I feel ripping pain followed by relief as the head comes fully out. "Yes, that's it, just the body left. Breathe deep, Sabine."

Rocking back and forth on my hands and knees with the women chatting around my naked form, I say his name over and over again in my head.

"Janus."

"Janus."

"Janus."

Giving one final deep, inward breath, I finally feel our child arrive, but something feels off.

My closed eyes open as I realise the chanting, my midwife and my baby are not making a sound. Not even a pin-drop can be heard.

"Cor animae meae," the words are spoken in a soft reverence, and my panic is forgotten. *He's here.* "She's here." I roll to lounge on the soft cushions next to me, finding my bronzed god kneeling before me, a tiny bundle of kicking limbs in his arms. Compared to Janus, our child looks minuscule in size.

Looking down at our baby, he grins wide, his eyes soft, his dark hair falling over his forehead. "She looks like you," he says in a hushed tone. Neither of us is willing to fully break this strange and alluring spell. The co-mingling of our love has brought us here. Janus gave me a baby. We have made life together, but he'll never be able to watch her grow.

Grabbing one of the baby blankets the midwife set aside, Janus deftly wraps our child up like he's been doing it all his life. Little gurgling sounds come from her lips, she barely fusses for him.

Finally, taking my eyes off the pair, I realise something has changed. "Where is ..." My midwife and the women sitting in the circle are still, silent, frozen in time.

Janus moves beside me, being careful to keep the umbilical cord freely flowing to our baby. "It will not last long." He sits down, moving his arm around my shoulder and pulling my naked body tight into his side. "It is just a trick of time. I'm only meant to use it for cataclysmic circumstances. I'd say my first child—my only child—is as close to cataclysmic as I'm going to get."

The heat of his body warms my side as he strokes his hand down my arm while he cradles our child close to his chest. I stare at him in awe, hardly able to string two words together. A pain rips through my lower half, and I crouch in on myself, holding my lower belly. The one thing I never lucked out on with the whole immortality thing is no pain. I get to feel every little thing that happens to my body; it just heals quickly. I tried to stab myself once, and that only left me in excruciating pain as the knife popped out of my body when the skin healed over itself. I guess, without pain, there would be no pleasure.

Turning to face me, Janus passes over the tiny bundle. "Hold onto her while I help you with the next part, cor animae meae." I nod as he passes the brown blanket over. Two amber eyes look up at me, with creamy fair skin and a sprinkling of dark mahogany hair.

"No, she looks like you." I choke out a laughing cry. Two wide eyes stare up at me. I place one of my fingers in her soft fist, giving her forehead a swift kiss, her baby smell melting me.

"Breathe in," Janus says as a hand pushes down on my lower stomach. I follow his instructions. "Breathe out," he concludes, releasing his hand, and out flows the last of the birth—a slight pressure, but nothing compared to before. I groan, easing back onto the pillows with my cute bundle.

"Bringer of life and death, and now a midwife. I'm impressed." I wink, and he smirks, crawling to lie beside us, giving me a soft kiss on the forehead, followed by our daughter.

"I missed you, Sabine. I'm sorry I could not come earlier." He clasps his broad hand around my left cheek and tilts my face to his. "Say you do not hate me."

I scowl, making the lines in his face deepen. "I'm surprised you didn't hear me cursing you out when I found out I was pregnant."

His fingers run a soothing line back and forth along my cheek. "I would've loved to have been there." Amber eyes lock on mine, telling me all his truths.

"How long can you stay for?" I ask, hoping it might be different this time. *It's his child. Surely, he has time for us now.*

A heavy sigh comes from his lips. "Technically, I should not be here. There was no door opening."

"What do you mean, no door opening? What about our baby?"

He chuckles—a secret I'm not quite privy to yet. "She was very eager, and entered your womb on conception." His finger smoothes her tiny cheek. My heart explodes at the small contact of seeing them together.

"What? How?" *I thought that souls entered at birth, not through the womb or by conception.*

"Souls enter their bodies whenever they feel it is the right time. Sometimes, that is in the womb. Sometimes, that is upon birth. That is why I am not present at all births, just all deaths."

"That makes so much sense." I grip the hand he has against my cheek. "I can't tell you how many births I've volunteered at for you to only show up at a few. It's why I've stuck to deaths." I meant to ask him that before, but we always seemed to get distracted.

"Smart girl." He reaches down, full lips landing on mine as he kisses me deeply. His hands find my hair pulling me closer to him, making me moan into his mouth. A steady pulse weaves down to my core, my body now fully healed after the birth. *Sometimes, this immortality thing is handy.*

A small squeak comes from between us, and we pull apart, looking at a pink face with chubby cheeks. "What should we call her?" I ask, my finger roaming over the smooth skin of her face, her little eyelids fluttering over her irises—the same shade as her father's.

"Amor." His deep tone moves me when he says the word like a secret only we know.

"Amor," I murmur. "Do you want to be called Amor, baby girl?" I ask.

She gazes up at us, her eyes catching on Janus. "She likes it," he says, his lips touching her forehead.

"Can you speak to babies now?" I ask, almost huffing that he has some type of connection with her I do not.

A soft rumble comes through his chest. "No, cor animae meae, I'm just a god who can speak to souls."

"Okay." I deflate and let his lips find mine. "Do you think she will be able to talk to souls, too, or is that just a you thing?"

"That is just a god thing, and our little Amor is human, as are you." I blanch, my heart giving way. It was filling, it was overflowing; we were so close to being a normal family, if only for a moment.

My stomach roils as I say, "But I'm not just a human. I'm immortal." I push the tiny girl in my arms towards Janus, silently begging him to take her, my eyes starting to fill with tears. A consequence of our actions finally falls into place. A realisation that I never wanted to confirm until now. "You must make her immortal too. You must make her a god." The dam in my eyes breaks as they spring free, concern etched fiercely into the perfectly sculpted face looking down at me. "I can't lose her. I can't ..." I choke, trying to push him back, but his free hand snakes around to crush our bodies together, my head burrowing a home in his chest. "Please. I thought she would be like you. You can't take her from me."

I didn't think it could hurt this much; the fear of her future. Seeing people die frequently has numbed me, but this new, fresh love for my baby—*our* baby—splits me wide open. My heart is bigger, but it isn't strong enough to handle her loss.

"Shhh, Sabine, all is well. I cannot give her my blood. It will stop her growth. Her soul has lived many lives. It is strong." I try to take comfort in his words, but I have seen too many children be taken by sickness or accident. I have nursed them through death to the inevitable door Janus opens. A small cry comes from between our bodies, making my limbs jolt in alarm. "She is just hungry." Janus runs his hand up and down my back, kissing my head.

As my heartbeat slows, he sits with us on the cushions while I feed Amor until she falls asleep in my arms.

He stares at her for a long time, just watching as she snuffles in her sleep, her little breaths hiccupping. "I must

go." His voice is quiet, barely audible like he doesn't want
to utter the words.

I want to plead with him to stay, but my heart no longer
has the energy. I have to be happy in the knowledge I
now have a piece of Janus with me always. Maybe our
time together was always leading to this. *When she's older,
perhaps he can feed her his blood.* But that thought quickly
turns sour. *No. I don't want her to be like me.* I don't want
her humanity to slowly slip away until life and death mean
nothing. Like a god, yet unable to go within the god realm.

Turning my face to his, he says, "You are the only thing
within both the mortal and immortal planes that gives me
joy, Sabine. You are the only reason I have a heart that
beats. When I found you bloody and broken, those men
..." He chokes, and I remember the look in his eyes that
night he found me, fury on his face. One of my attackers
had killed one of the others because they had plundered
me first. That's how he came to be standing over me, a
god of vengeance, my death angel. He ended their souls—a
one-way ticket to the Underworld, never to grace Earth's
surface again. Then, he cradled me in his arms as I pleaded
with him. "When I found you, my heart found its beat
again. You gave me life. You made me see the beauty in

wanting to live. That day, I wished I was but a mere man who could spend his days loving you until his last breath, but I was also glad I wasn't a mortal. For the first time, I was happy to be a god because I could save you. It was selfish, keeping you. Immoral. Against all the rules. But I would do it again in a heartbeat, cor animae meae."

His lips descend on mine, and we kiss until I'm breathless, his tongue taking great sweeps of my own, lapping up every last drop of my essence before he is gone. *Crack.* The echo vibrates the fabric walls of the tent as chanting springs back to life, and I look down at the impossibility in my arms.

Summoning Pluto

Present Day, 9th June, 2025 AD

I figure if I want to get into the Underworld, I need a really bad soul. Someone so terrible he will bleed black. I say *he* because I'm not into killing women. Yeah, I know, souls don't discriminate between genders, but I just feel a certain sense of feminine justice after past wrongs when I find myself with a knife to the throat of a man—especially one who rapes women.

There was one time in history when I seduced the Roman emperor, Nero, to take back my failing empire. It was 59 AD. To gain his ear, I had to kill his mother. She was a snake of a woman who sought to control her son until her dying breath. I just made that happen sooner rather than later.

But, for the most part, I always find myself killing men.

I spend some time in the closest city, Edinburgh, scouting out the local talent. I've spent thousands of years playing this game. All it takes is one look, and I can tell if they are a bad seed, so to speak. When this grey-eyed motherfucker looks at me from across the bar, wedding ring line on his finger, tweaking eyes and just general cocky demeanour, I pounce, batting my eyelashes.

"Hey, baby, need another drink?" He barely finishes the question before he's plonking himself on the barstool next to me. I found myself drawn to a swanky business bar attached to an upper-class hotel that seems to attract men in suits. My victim is suited up, his eyes lingering on my breasts, which I've hoisted up into a black corset top, my hair flowing effortlessly in waves down my back, minimal makeup on to showcase my youth. I've barely been here five minutes, and I've already reeled in a sucker.

I smile shyly at him, and he takes that at his cue to order two dirty martinis. *So fucking original.* My eyes practically roll into the back of my head.

"So, what's a pretty little thing like you doing out all alone on a Friday night?" *Here we go. The story.*

I sniffle a bit for dramatic effect and lower my lashes, wringing my hands on the bar. "My boyfriend just broke up with me. He has been sleeping with my best friend, and I thought ..." I trail off, hoping he fills in the blanks.

His sweaty palm finds my trembling fingers. *Gross.* "You want to make him jealous, baby?" *Baby? Double gross.*

Biting my lip, I look up at him and laugh softly. "I was hoping I might find someone to ... You know, maybe take some pictures with and send them to him. He hates when other guys flirt with me."

Having the all-clear that I'm still fully hung up on my ex and just need some quick fun, Sweaty Palms jumps in headfirst. "Looks like we found each other at the right time. My wife just left me for another guy." *Doubtful.* I groan inwardly. "And I'd love to take you up to my room to make your boyfriend jealous." He smirks, and I down my drink.

"You have more alcohol up in your room ...?" I look closely at him, squinting my eyes. He looks like a William or something prim and proper. A bit like Grayson, but Gray would never have been this sleazy.

"Brandon." Bile rises in my throat as he says his name, but, playing the part, I smile and shake his hand. "Sure do. Let's go, pretty lady." He pulls me up with outstretched hands and shouts at the bartender to put our drinks on his t ab. *Asshole.*

Once we make it to his room, I flop onto his bed, directing him to make me a stiff drink. I have every faith that he'll roofie it for me.

Sitting up on the bed, I take in the surroundings of the spacious room. When we were in the elevator, he mentioned he had a suite. I was unimpressed. Like most men, he seems to think money is the way into my underwear, but I have much higher standards. *God or bust.* I giggle at myself, pushing my body up to see Mister Sweaty Palms Brandon heading my way with two tumblers in hand.

I've been married to an emperor, frolicked in harems, fought in wars and assassinated major figures in society. I won't name names, but I feel like I should get a parade for all the filth I've cleaned off the streets. I've been a professor, written books, stolen priceless artwork. Don't forget the time I got shot, and in between healing, was caught, put in a cell and had to facilitate my own jail break. The not being able to die thing is very handy whenever you need to get out of a situation. I've experienced life this piece of scum could never fathom with his puny pea brain. And you know how I know he's a piece of scum? Because the glass he hands me still has trace amounts of a powdery substance floating around in it, while his is calm and still. *Scum.*

Grabbing the tumbler full of a brown liquor, I pretend to give it the smallest of sips, smiling up at him. He takes a large swig of his, and as soon as he's done, I pull myself up and grasp his cup to place them on the bedside table.

"Don't you want to finish your drink?" His eyes linger towards the two glasses as I shake my head, my fingers tracing up his navy button-down.

"Mmm, I think we should get to the good part." My voice is a whisper.

"Fuck yeah we should." He clamps his arms around my waist and squeezes my arse, the black leather miniskirt I'm wearing riding up.

"Not yet." I waggle my eyebrows at him, pushing away to reach for my bag. "We need evidence." I pull my phone out of the small clutch I brought with me. Eyeing my body as it moves over the sheets, he doesn't protest as he unbuttons his shirt. Handing him the phone—open to my camera—I say in the softest voice I can manage, flipping my long auburn hair over my shoulder, trailing a finger over the curves of my upper chest, "Maybe you could take some pictures of me sucking your cock? I think that would make my ex really jealous." I giggle at the end for effect.

"Jesus, baby, you can suck whatever you want." His eyes drop in lust at my words, taking snap after snap of my body inching back over to the bedside table to grab our drinks. Manoeuvring so he can't see me swapping them, I edge off the bed and walk over to him, handing him the spiked drink. I down my own quickly so he barely notices the difference in contents, and he takes his without complaint, downing it in one swig. *Idiot.*

I can't help the wide smile that carves my face. I sink to my knees before him, telling him to sit on the edge of the bed. Running my hands up and down his weedy thighs, I say, "Thank you for helping me out. I wasn't sure I could do this."

His fingers find my hair, making my body shrivel inward. The smell of him is beyond reproach as lingering wafts of body odour and cologne hit my nose, making me want to gag. But I've had worse.

Shifting my fingers up towards his pant zipper, I can feel him hard already. I hesitate. "I ..." I look up at him, biting on my bottom lip. "I don't know if I can do this," I exhale softly, his hands finding mine, encouraging me to open his zipper.

"Of course you can. Just imagine how much it will piss off your ex. He'll hate seeing you suck on a big cock like mine."

Releasing my bottom lip, I whimper, "Do you think?"

His eyes start to blink slowly, and he takes an unhurried lick of his lips. *Just in time. I really didn't want to have to suck rotten cock.* "Yeah, of course, baby. He'll hate it." Pulling my hand down the zipper, I stop. He shakes his head. "Fuck, baby, come on." He starts to get impatient with me, pulling my hair tighter.

"You're not holding up the phone," I say, raising my eyebrows.

"Shit. Right." He fumbles with the device he'd dropped earlier next to his leg, but quickly finds himself unable to hold it up, his whole body losing strength. "Fuck, I—thi—n—k I do—ne drunk toooo muuuccchh," he gets out before I push his chest, making him flop back onto the bed just as his eyes close.

"Too easy," I tell him, standing back up. The male species is becoming too predictable with time, but so are the women. *Gods, if Pluto doesn't take me to the Underworld, I will just find a god that will take me from Earth.* My soul is exhausted from this place.

Pulling the dagger out of my heeled boot, I lean over Brandon's body. "Time to meet your maker, you piece of shit," I scowl as I slam the blade right into his chest. I'm careful to sink it between the bones so I barely hit any resistance going down, blood slowly pooling to the surface and seeping into his shirt. I contemplate making this a messier affair—maybe cutting his dick off—but the thought of his rancid blood on me gives me hives, and I want to look my best for Pluto ... Or maybe ... *Janus.*

Now, I wait.

I pull back and sit next to the gurgling body. After cleaning the dagger on the bedsheets, I place it back into my boot.

He said he wouldn't come again. He said it was the last time, so let's hope my only other chance at freedom finds me.

A sizzling sensation moves over my skin, making the tiny hairs on my arms stand on end. *No one is coming.*

No *crack.*

No Roman god angered with me.

No Roman god desperate for my lips.

Just as I'm about to give up, a rush of warm air wafts over my body, my eyes finding dark, tanned skin stretched over sinewy muscle, like Janus but not, standing only a few feet before me. This god wears a black, leather-strapped skirt decorated in gold, hanging low on his well-defined hips, so close to nearly exposing all of him. *Is he even wearing underwear under that, or is it just all hanging out? One slight move and those leather straps draped from his hips could reveal everything.*

The sound of a throat clearing hits my ears, my eyes fly up to find a darker shade of amber eyes than Janus's and white, curled hair, framing strong, harsh features, a white beard covering his lips.

My heart fissures, my hand involuntarily reaching for it. *He didn't come. He finally gave up on us.*

Shit. I didn't think it would hurt this bad, but I can't help the reactions of my human body as agony barrels through my chest, my breath wheezing out of me.

I don't even care if this other god is bearing witness to my inner crumbling, my body folding over as I place my head between my legs. I was all bravado, saying I wanted

Pluto to show up. Secretly, I wished Janus would come back to me. That he would find me again. That we would just have one more perfect moment in this shitty existence I've been playing out.

"Can you see me?" a rough voice asks. *Pretty reasonable question, really.* Sandalled feet make their way over to me, the god standing inches before me now. I see his toes out of the top of my cocooned position. A deep growl emanates from his chest before large hands come to grip my body and effortlessly lift me up. "LOOK AT ME," his voice blasts through my ears, making my body open from its shell, hanging limp before him. My feet dangle, his grip holding me firmly in front of his eyes. "HOW?" he roars, like I'm just meant to understand what this god is talking about.

His bearded face scowls at me, his eyes firing from the cores, making the amber even more darkly brilliant than before. A rumbling comes through his chest, and I smell smoke wafting off his skin like a bonfire. "Why do you smell like him?"

Like the piece of shit in the bed? I rack my brain for a second until I understand his meaning. *Right. Janus.* His one drop of blood living inside of me, keeping me from dying, keeping me from living, my soul in eternal limbo.

"Janus?" I question because I know he knows, and who knows what he's going to do with that information.

"JANUS," he roars as he throws my body onto the bed. I land against a very dead Brandon, and I slink away, rubbing at my chest.

"I need you to take me with you to the Underworld." May as well get straight to the point. I know he doesn't have time to stick around and talk to humans. God rule number one: don't let the humans see you. I know once Janus saved me, he never showed himself to another human again. Apparently, too much meddling in the early days brought about too much death and destruction, so the gods decided they would no longer show themselves.

The god before me roams back and forth, wearing a path in the carpet. "He knows the rules. He helped make the rules. No fucking humans. No more fucking humans. And he gives blood to one of them."

"Just to me," I pipe up, hoping that may help. *As far as I know, just to me. Surely, he hasn't done this to another. He wouldn't. Would he? No, not after Amor.* I go to stand, but Pluto points a finger at me and tells me to sit like I'm some petulant child. Sitting on my arse, I bounce a few times and continue, "My name is Sabine. In 752 BC, Janus gave me a drop of his blood when I pleaded with him to save me. I ..."

Fire-filled eyes turn to me, orange rings of flames show-casing his anger as the god's hands tense by his sides. "You're telling me you have been walking the earthly plains for nearly 3,000 years?" It is more than a question; it is an accusation. I nod my head, not knowing how to respond. "Do you realise what he has done?" This time, I shake my head. "He is at risk of losing his power. Of being sent to Tartarus. If the others knew of you ..." The god slows his pacing and stands before me with his hands on his hips, fuming at his discovery. "He always liked the human world too much, asking me to help him, never explaining why. This goes too fucking far."

Turning, the god before me ends his monologue, going to leave. I panic. "Don't leave. I need to come with you."

The tall, imposing man stops. I trail my eyes over the well-defined muscles of his back, white hair falling to his shoulders.

Suddenly turning faster than I can blink, he has me pinned to the bed next to Brandon. His broad form looms over me, orange eyes burning into my soul, seeking an-swers. Wide fingers flex over my throat, and he whispers menacingly, "Do you think I will save you, whore?" he spits the word into my face. "I know your kind. Janus is too blind to see past a pretty smile and a tight cunt, but I have no use for such things. I will feed on your soul and keep it rotting for eternity within my flames."

My heart races, pushing to be free, regretting the words I am to say next, but I say them anyway, rage spurring me on. Rage for Janus, rage for the men who hurt me in this life and rage for being stuck in time. "Take it then," I rasp out. "Take my soul. TAKE ..." I try to squeeze out, but he holds my throat tighter.

He laughs right in my face, spicy smoke lingering on my senses at his nearness. His teeth gleam as he says, "You will regret saying those words."

I want to ask why, but before I can utter a word, my stomach swoops, and I'm no longer lying on a hotel bed.

Blinking to shake the strange fog out of my head, I pale at the feel of silken sheets beneath me. Pushing my throat into the mattress, he lets me go and stands before a dark, wooden four-poster bed, glaring down at me, ire a heavy mask encasing his masculine features.

Little black dots dance in my periphery. I know just from the smell of heavy ash in the air that we are no longer in the hotel room. Ignoring the swirling in my gut, I look around, seeing grey stone walls, a large, open fireplace with roaring flames and frosted leadlight windows, glowing red.

Are we here? Are we in the Underworld?

My brain short-circuits for a second, unable to believe this worked.

I hear heavy footfalls striding towards the other side of the room, my heart thumping erratically as I realise he's going to leave. "Hey, where are you—"

The door slams, and I'm alone.

Now that I'm here, I feel paralysed with uncertainty about what is going to happen next.

Vale

The Past, 1944 AD

*P*op. The sound of a bullet travels through another skull—another soldier put out of his misery as he twists in agony on the killing fields. *Such a fucking waste.*

"Sabine." Two hands grab my body from behind, I pull the trigger on a poor bastard covered in dirt and blood. "Sabine, stop."

My body is pulled into a warm chest, my feet fly off the ground and a nose nuzzles into the back of my neck. Salty seas coat the back of my throat, though I don't want to acknowledge it—or him.

I can't stop. This is pointless. This war is senseless. All these men, killing for power. For land. For money. It makes no sense to me. I've lived thousands of years of this unbelievable cruelty. The least I can do is put these souls out of their misery, so I aim and shoot again.

"SABINE, STOP!" the voice moves through my sinew, my trigger hand falls, the gun still firmly in my grasp, just in case.

"I'm not doing this for you. I'm doing this for me, for them." I wave my hand around at the dead bodies lying before us on muddy, open lands—boys and men killing each other for unknown entities that hide behind their fancy cars and mansions. My blood boils with rage for what this world is turning into. It's always been bad, but I thought maybe we were making progress. It seems not.

"I know. Fuck ... Cor meum, pausa."

"No," I growl.

His chest rumbles at my back. "We cannot do this anymore. You need to find peace in this world. I cannot watch on as you waste away in this place."

The heat of his words cleaves my chest as he crushes my back to his front. "There is no peace for me here, Janus. You know this." A bomb lands to my right, I flinch.

"We cannot do this here. I have souls to deliver," he grits out.

"Leave me, then. That's all you're good for, isn't it, cor animae meae?" He stiffens behind me. *Good, I struck a nerve.* I'm a fire, and I have no time to think about the consequences of my words or how they affect the god behind me. *He's a god, for fuck's sake. He can deal with my petty human emotions.*

"If I could, I would serve this world to you on a platter, or I would burn everything to ash if it were in my power. Your pain brings me pain for the first time in my existence, and I have no idea what to do but bow at your feet and hope that, one day, you will forgive me. I'm yours infinitus. I only hope that is enough. Vale, cor animae meae." The words are anguished, some broken by gunshots.

He releases me, vanishing out of sight, and I fall on my hands and knees. "No," I whisper. My hands dig deep into the dirt beneath me, smoke filling my lungs. My heart is swollen—a throbbing that moves throughout my limbs. "No VALE, NO GOODBYE!" I scream in anger at my hands. A thick ball in my throat chokes me with this new pain. *He's never ... He's never said goodbye before. He can't tell me I'm his everything, then tell me goodbye.*

"ARRRRRRRRRRR—" I scream again amidst sounds of war, my own battle raging in my heart. I pound my fists on the ground. *For once, I wish I could leave him.*

Cracked Open

The Past, 1944 AD

Soul after soul flashes before my eyes as I continue ushering them from the mortal plane of existence. But I cannot get her out of my head. Ever since I saved her all those millennia ago, she's been a permanent fixture on my soul, burnt in, etched for eternity. A fierce reverence. The only soul who has ever caught my attention. I couldn't even tell you exactly what it was that sucked me in. When those blistering blue-green eyes locked onto mine, it was the first time I felt time stop. For once, I wasn't just a god who ushered in life and death. I felt like more. Like this human woman was my salvation. Sabine was a compass I sought out time and time again. She was my humanity when I lacked an understanding as a god. And I ruined her. After Amor passed over, I was sure she would hate me, and she did ... for a while.

The memory of our sweet daughter is never far from my mind. It flickers constantly, forever reminding me why I should stay away, keep my distance.

A door for death is what drew me to them. I never open up to what I'm entering into until I'm there, and even then, it is of no concern as long as the souls I'm helping are ushered through the portals. As long as their lights end up where they need to go, I look no further. But the smell of roses tore at my heart, and I stopped just to see if it was her.

I'd taken to spying on her more and more through my mind's eye when I wasn't ushering souls, but I hadn't checked on them in a while, which was the biggest mistake of my existence.

I was not prepared for what I saw.

Pain—or what I thought must be pain—moved through my chest cavity and up my throat as I looked upon Sabine and Amor sitting peacefully under a large oak tree near a wooden cottage. Rows of garden beds surrounded the cottage, no doubt food for our child.

Tears streamed down pale cheeks as I stepped towards Sabine. She clutched a large bundle of blankets to her chest, rocking back and forth slowly.

"Don't." Her voice was gruff and harsh as she spoke the word to me. "You did this."

It was a knife's edge twisting into my soul, and she knew it. Sabine wanted to hurt me like she was hurting. If she only knew the pain I felt seeing her for the first time amongst those Roman soldiers. She cracked me wide open, and I've never been able to put the pieces back together again.

She only had eyes for the small form she cradled. I knew by the dark, wispy hair and pert, full lips who she held precious in her arms. The small face, still rounded with youth.

I wanted to scream for her. It wasn't meant to happen that way—an accident. It took Amor from us too young.

As I dropped to my knees, I'd never felt more helpless in my life. I couldn't save our child. Despite what humans may choose to believe, the gods cannot predict death; that is up to the fates, and they are beyond us. We just orchestrate their grand plans. And I wanted to rip the world apart for their decision to take my daughter away.

Feeding her my blood wasn't an option. Her body was no longer alive. Her soul was ready to pass through the door. Having her become immortal at such a young age was unthinkable. It was already eating at Sabine, her humanity slipping away with each century.

All that was left was a body my heart clutched onto for dear life.

It was at that moment—seeing Sabine falling apart, my own psyche rupturing beyond repair—that I knew I had to truly distance myself from her.

No more meetings, no more sweet nothings, no more lovemaking.

That day was the day I realised everything had to change. My love for Sabine grew beyond my own need. It grew into something intangible. I became her protector.

We didn't share any more words, but as I sat with her under that oak tree, she found space in my open arms, and we gazed upon our daughter together for the second time. I helped her create a pyre so she didn't have to do it alone.

My chest ached with the thought that she would be on her own when I left. So, after her tears spilt and she shared wondrous stories of our daughter's life, I asked her to go find love again without me. I told her she was free of me. That I wanted her to find love in each lifetime. I didn't want her to be without.

I couldn't give her a life where I was forever at her side. I was a god, and I would forever be so, chained to my duties.

I implored her to live for me if she couldn't live for herself. Amor would return again and again, but Sabine was forever stuck because of me.

If I ever said I regretted giving her my blood, it would be a lie. The only thing I truly regret is leaving her.

And now I'm doing it again, here on this battlefield. I just told her goodbye like it was the last time. Like I'll never watch her.

Cor animae meae, all I do is watch you. Do you not feel how you carry my heart around in your chest? I've burdened her for too long. I cannot risk her being known to the other gods. The only possible place I can bring her to is the Underworld, and I will never take her there. To him. He may be my nephew, but Pluto is unhinged. He will torture her soul for eternity. Pluto deplores humans more than any other god.

I will have to hope that giving her my heart is enough.
She is everything to me. *Fates, have mercy on me.*

The Underworld

Present Day, 9th-10th June, 2025 AD

The door is locked, and the windows are sealed shut. I guess I shouldn't have expected anything less from the god of the Underworld; captured in a pretty prison of luxury. I should be glad my soul's not burning in Tartarus, and I somehow have a warm, comfy bed to rest my head. Maybe this *is* Tartarus, and it's more of a mind game situation, like they somehow beat you down with mental trickery. Joke's on Pluto, though, because I've spent thousands of years perfecting my mental prowess—unless he brings up Janus. Then, I may lose it. And since he knows my weakness, he'll probably use it against me.

"Just how fucked am I?" I ask the walls, sort of hoping I'll get an answer back.

A squeaking comes from the door, making me jump. I hold my hand to my chest as Pluto strides into the room, his all-encompassing presence shrinking the space, making it seem smaller than it is.

"Sit," he commands, his thick fingers pointing towards the black leather sofa by the fire—one of those ones that has the brass studs along the armrests. Not wanting to sit, instead choosing to keep my vigil by the fire, makes the god growl ominously under his breath, "Sit."

His eyes glow orange at my blatant disrespect for him. A chill washes over my skin, but that soon dissipates as my own fire springs true. I'm too far gone for a god or the possibility of eternal death to scare me. I've experienced pain this god will never understand.

He will not get to me.

Pinning me with his eyes, Pluto now stands before me, anger laced in his soul. *Good thing we both have angry souls.* The thought makes me smile, which seems to aggravate the god further. His hand shoots out to take mine, his vice grip crushing my fingers, bone grinding against bone.

"Do not be so flippant with my hospitality, human. I can snap your bones without a single thought." To prove his point, his grip only gets tighter. I wince. A throbbing works its way up my arm.

"Break it, I dare you," I spit the words out, my face angled up to see him, his perfectly groomed ivory beard catching any lingering saliva that comes flying his way.

Crunch. The sound isn't so much heard through my ears as it is felt through my body. All the bones in my hand turn to dust. I've done worse before, but that does not stop the pain from lancing through me, making darkness move across my sight, a whimper leaving my lips as I squeeze my eyes shut.

Gruff hairs tickle my ear. Pluto moves in close, whispering, "I can tell I'm going to have fun with you, but first, you promised me something."

Somehow finding my strength, Janus's blood knits my bones back together easing the ache in my hand. I grit out, "What?"

"Your soul." *Oh, shit. That.*

Harshly taking my jaw in his hand, my skin bruising under his touch, Pluto brings our lips together. "Tell me it's mine."

It's not his. It belongs to Janus. But if it's the only way to get me out of this place, he can have it. I'm done. "Sure, you can have it."

"Fucking human," he grumbles, then puts his lips to mine, pulling deeply, sucking down my air.

Until, suddenly, he stops. His head flinches back as if he has been burnt. Pushing me away from him, he grasps my head between his hands, twisting it, a sickening snap ringing in my ears and the words "*Fucking Janus*" rumbling through my disoriented mind. I sink into nothingness.

"Human, human," a flickering voice calls to me through the darkness. "Wake up." Something shakes my arm as I find myself lying on a hard surface.

My eyelids flutter open to find wide green eyes staring back at me from a beautiful, heart-shaped face, golden hair falling to touch my chest. I reach my hand to touch the shining locks, finding them smooth and silky.

"Good, you're awake." Her smile is slight as she sits back on her heels, fine, golden tendrils slipping through my grasp. "I was concerned he had killed you. He doesn't have much patience for your kind. But when I came in and found your heart still beating, I knew you were different." The slight smile kicks up a notch, and I can't help but replicate it.

Pulling my full body to sit next to her, I rub at the phantom twinge in my neck from where Pluto snapped it. I must admit that was a first. I've been shot, stabbed, set on fire, but I've never had my neck snapped.

"Here, drink this." The golden-haired woman hands me a glass of red liquid. I shake my head.

"I don't need it," I say. The thought of drinking or eating right now fills me with dread.

Her face washes with disappointment, but it soon crosses with a curious gleam to her eyes as she studies me, whispering, "So it's true. Janus gave you his blood?"

At the mention of him, I move my hand from my head to the cavity in my chest. That pesky organ still beats for the god of beginnings and endings after millennia. "Yes. He found me dying a long time ago."

Eyes bugging, she asks, "You're talking about bronzed Janus, right? He has dark hair, about this length"—she holds her hands to her ears—"sharp cheekbones, a perpetual scowl and is impossibly tall."

She tilts her head as if trying to gage a read on me. Everything about the description sounds spot on except for the perpetual scowl. That depends on his mood—or mine—and how I push his buttons. The thought of that makes me smile. *Stop thinking about Janus. He left you, Sabine,* I chide myself.

"That sounds like him."

"Wowwww." The word is stretched out as she says it, her lips rounded, almost gaping open. "No wonder he's angry." The last part is a whisper.

"Who's angry? Pluto?" I question. He's the only other person I've met in this place.

Her features glaze over for a second before she whips her head back to me. "Don't concern your pretty head about it." She grabs my hand. "Do you want to be friends?"

Not knowing if I have any other options in this situation, I nod my head.

"Oh, yay! I don't have many friends down here. Some-times, the other gods come to visit Pluto, but that's all." She stares into the flames of the fireplace.

"What's your name? I'm Sabine," I say, realising I haven't asked this woman who she is.

"Proserpina, but you can call me Pina." She clutches my hand tight.

"I'm glad to have a friend down here, Pina," I reply. Her childlike smile is infectious. We grin widely at each other. Besides Janus, I've never known another immortal creature. My heart does a little gallop.

"Now that we are friends, I have to tell you a secret." Her voice turns down several octaves. I move in closer to her.

"Okay?" *What secrets could she need to spill to a relative stranger? She did say she had no friends.*

"Pluto wants to kill you."

A bubbling laughter works its way up my throat. "Hate to break it to you, Pina, but he already tried that. It's impossible. I have Janus's blood."

Her sweet face turns into a sneer, her grip going tight as she adds, "Pluto is deceptive. He—"

Crack. A gush of air moves over us, knocking out the fire. Pina is ripped from my grasp. Demanding words pierce the air around us. "What have I told you, Proserpina? Stay within your wing." Venom flows from Pluto as he holds the top of Pina's arms in his grasp, her bare feet kicking out below her emerald green dress.

He shoves his face in hers until her gaze lowers to her feet. "I'm sorry, Pluto. I just thought we could be friends."

"Friends," he laughs, loud and obnoxious. "Proserpina, you are mine. You need no friends." Chucking her over his shoulder like a rag doll, he slaps her arse, making her yelp.

"Now for you, human." He crooks a finger at me. "Crawl to me."

I baulk at his command. "What?"

Smirking, shadows sweep the room, all the remaining flickers of flame dissipate, my head spinning with a feeling I haven't felt in a long time. Not since Amor. Fear. "Girl, I am your master now, and you will do as I demand, or I will throw you into Tartarus with the rest of the leeches."

Pina doesn't move a muscle, she lies over the broad shoulder of the god, his anger palpable through his thick beard. The air smells of ash, like the small flickers of my heart. I don't want to fear this god. He can't kill me, though ending up in the fiery pits of hell makes me question my current choices. *Did I make a mistake coming here? I should've listened to Janus—*

"This is your last warning, girl. If you don't crawl to me now, I'll kill your precious god."

"What?" My eyes flick up to the sneering immortal. He knows my weakness. Sure, the thought of Tartarus scares me, but it's just me. It's not affecting anyone else. I can handle it. *I hope I can handle it. But Janus, he—*a ball lands heavy in my throat. "You can't kill another god," I call his bluff.

Producing an onyx dagger from his leather shirt, he twirls it in his fingers. "You're right. I may not be able to, but you can." He throws the blade towards me. My mind blanks, unable to comprehend what he is saying.

Taking a heavy breath, Pluto points towards the sharp dagger. "What are you, dumb, girl? Pick up the fucking blade."

Licking my lips, I find my voice. "I don't understand."

"Fucking humans. Idiots, the lot of you," he groans, storming towards me. "Pick. Up. The. Dagger." He punctuates each of the words as if I'm deaf. My hands shake on my knees. I look towards the offending piece of black cr ystal. *Is it magic? Surely, nothing can kill Janus. Nothing can kill the gods. They are eternal. They are beyond the creation of life and death.* A heavy palm whacks against my cheek, making me fall towards the floor. My mind rings with a heavy headache, a metallic taste floating past my lips. "If you continue to ignore my commands, girl, I'll send her soul to Tartarus."

My ears ring as I push my body off the floor. *What did he say? Her? This psycho is just spouting random shit now. Great, I summoned a complete moron—worse than the ones on Earth. I should've listened to Janus. I'll never live this down.*

A hand comes to yank my head to face angered eyes. "Did you hear me, slut? I have her. You and Janus thought you could hide her from me, but nothing can be hidden from the god of the Underworld."

My eyes roll into the back of my head at his crazed words. I swipe at my mouth, red blood staining my lips as I try to speak. "I don't know"—I cough and try again—"I don't know who you are talking about."

"No?" His smirks condescendingly. I don't know what he's expecting of me, but there's no one on Earth I have attachments to anymore. Slowly, my body starts to mend itself together, the pain in my cheek diminishing to be taken over by the agony from where he's yanking at my head. *Fucking prick.* If he was human, I could evade his hold, but I'm not stupid. I'm no match for a god's powers. "Let me show you, slut." Pluto yanks me roughly to my feet. The ache in my skull radiates through my vertebrae, my mouth greedily sucking in air to stem the pain until Janus's blood heals any rips he makes.

Pluto teleports us from my darkened room. Adjusting my eyes to the unexpected sensation of my body moving through space, I blink a few times as I'm thrown on the floor again, knees roughly hitting the hard stone beneath. I want to curse the ancient fucker out, but I can't seem to bring myself to spill my anger when he's holding secrets over me.

Regaining some semblance of control over my body, I look up to find myself in some sort of grand dining hall, complete with wrought iron chandeliers and an exquisite black marble table. My skirt rides up my thighs, and I pull it down grabbing hold of a heavy iron chair. I push up, noticing large windows overlooking a dusty red sky opposite me. The sight baffles me as I gravitate towards the unusual vista. The view from my bedroom is blocked through frosted glass, so this new visual is utterly bewildering and, to be honest, an interesting change of pace.

Before I can reach the sight to find out what my future might look like in the Underworld, a muffled sound catches my attention. Tilting my head to the side, I see a woman strapped to one of those heavy chairs lining the dining table. Her brown eyes are wide with fear. They look at me pleadingly. *What the fuck sort of game is Pluto playing at?*

My eyes find the indomitable god at the head of the table, a pliant Pina sitting to his right. He takes a casual pose in his chair, almost like he's waiting for me to realise something.

Taking a deep lungful of air, I ask, "What is going on, Pluto? Who is this?" I take another look at the woman, worried crinkles pulling at the sides of her eyes, black, shoulder-length hair hanging loose. I have never seen this woman before, and I go to tell Pluto as much, but he beats me to it.

"Maybe take a closer look." The instinct to know more is there, so, taking a step to the other side of the table, I peer closer at the woman giving me beseeching eyes. I lean towards her, and she starts to make panicked, muffled sounds behind the leather gag Pluto must have placed in her mouth. She looks to be in her thirties—technically older than me when I was immortalised—but the closer I stare at her eyes, the more something familiar churns in my mind, or is it my heart? There's something about this woman. Something I know.

A nervous giggle comes from the head of the table, and I see Pina with a glass of red liquid. *Where did that come from?* Pluto tips his own glass to his lips. "Look at that, Pina, she truly doesn't know. Sabine, don't tell me you don't recognise your own daughter?"

Like a punch to the gut or the tearing of my heart, the recognition behind this woman's eyes hits me.

Let her go, Sabine. You must let her soul go back to the eternal so she may enter in new forms. Amor doesn't belong to us. She was made from love, but her essence is her own. Let her be free.

Janus's words hit me worse than the slap to the face Pluto gave me. I've searched for her soul. I've waited for her to return to Earth. Year after year, I've searched, but I am no god, and Janus refused to help me. *She doesn't belong to us,* he would remind me. I used to get so angry at him. In those days, I wondered why he didn't try to throw me in Tartarus himself. All I was was fury.

Closing my eyes, letting my chest rise and fall, I say the words that kill me, "I don't know this woman."

Give Me More

The Past, 22 AD

I could try to find a birth, but they are not guaranteed. So, instead, I find myself tailing an older couple through the cobbled streets. I'm not happy with my choice, but this is what desperation looks like. Janus leaves me no other choice. At least they will go together.

Pulling my cloak over my shoulders, I slink behind a pillar as they stop in front of an arched doorway. The couple live in one of the nicer quarters of the city, so when their families or neighbours find them, it won't be too much of a surprise. I'll take some pieces that will be good for trading. Robberies are commonplace in the wealthier parts of the city.

Once I'm in their bedroom, I wait for the soft rise and fall of their chests to even out. It's a hot night, so the bedroom windows are wide open to the elements. *I'll have to be careful of any noise carrying.*

Sidling over to the bed, I poise my dagger over the woman's chest, aiming for just the right spot to achieve a killing blow. Quickly covering her mouth with my other hand, I plunge downward. She's a small woman, like me, but I have youth and god blood on my side, so after an initial gasp and some body-twitching, she's gone. I move up onto the bed, placing myself over the husband, and aim for his chest and twist, making quick work of the slightly bigger man. He bucks, making a strangled, screaming sound, but he's gone before I hear the first *crack* of Janus entering my murder scene.

Breathing heavily, I wait for the god to take in what I've done. Angry footfalls are upon me before I take my next breath or extract my simple but effective steel dagger from the elderly man's chest.

Two hands fall upon my body, lifting me up and spinning me around to be crushed against an unforgivingly hard but warm, golden chest. Dark chest hairs tickle my fingers as I revel in running my hands over his body, sucking in anything he can give me.

"Why are you doing this, Sabine?" Janus's voice is gruff and demanding. His hands band around my waist, crushing my body to his, almost leaving me breathless. *Gods, if he could just merge our bodies together, I would be content with this existence.* Wiggling my body, Janus groans, laying his chin on the top of my head.

"I miss you," I say, running my hands around his neck to grasp him tighter. It's true, I do miss him. I miss him like a piece of my heart is stolen from me every time he disappears into thin air. My body aches for his touch. I've spent many hours dreaming of us together, a normal couple strolling along the banks of the winding rivers, hand in hand. I thought, when Amor left this world, I'd eventually be okay. That time would heal me, knowing her soul was safe to be free. But every day, my heart breaks for everything I missed when she died as a child. I want to try again. I want more from this life. I need something to love in the tangible. And Janus can give that to me again. I know he c an.

"Sabine," he grumbles as I tickle the back of his neck and nibble across his jawline. His hands grip me tighter.

"Janus, just tonight. Please, cor animae meae." When I say those words, he breaks, and our lips meet, the two bodies on the bed forgotten to this one moment we get together. Maybe this sounds harsh, but they get to live again, they get to try again. This is all I get. Janus is my ending. I don't get any more beginnings. I'd kill them all to get to him.

"Cor animae meae, you have me. You have all of me," he grunts, pulling back, his lips rubbing across mine as he speaks. "If I were not bound to my godly duties, I would live every moment with you, basking in your glory."

"Is there not a way you can break free?" A question I've asked before, but I will continue to ask it until I get an answer I like.

His lip twitches, amber eyes burning into mine. Two strong hands come up to cup my cheeks. "You, my love, are the only person who sees me. Who understands the cage I've been placed in. The prison that keeps me from you." His forehead presses against mine, my legs wrapping around his midsection. Warmth radiates through my body at his proximity, a familiar heat travelling to my core and pure masculinity filling my senses. "I never thought I'd experience love like the humans do. Love that requires sacrifice. Love that requires patience. Love that takes over your whole body and soul. Love without conditions. Love that drives you crazy. It was the only part of the human existence I envied. And then I found you, my sweet cor animae meae." A searing kiss finds my lips, melting me further into his broad frame. "You are everything to me. If I could take all your suffering, I would."

"Then take it," I say, muffling my last words as I latch back onto his lips. Strong, sweeping licks make my body pool with need.

I know he can smell me like a siren song to his raging cock—the one I feel firmly pressed to my midsection, drapes of toga fabric keeping it from its destination.

Crack.

I shriek at the sudden sound and movement of our bodies, my heart swiftly picking up speed within my chest. "Look at me, Sabine." His voice moves around me. A shiver runs through my form, realising I'm still safely nestled within his arms, but in a new location.

My eyes find him, my whole world is condensed into his brilliant irises. *I just want to die and live in his universe for eternity. Is that so much to ask?*

"What can I do to make it better?" His broad fingers stroke my cheek lovingly.

I fall into his palm. "Give me another baby?"

Janus's back stiffens, his hand pressing firmly down on the underside of my jaw, bringing our faces together so I cannot hide from him. *Good. I do not want to hide anymore. I want him to see how much I need this. How much I want this. Even if it is crazy.*

We stare, our eyes transfixed on the other, worlds colliding.

His body starts to vibrate underneath mine until I see his frown smooth out into resignation. "You know what the answer I must give you is, Sabine. I wish you would not ask things of me I cannot give. I would tear the world apart to see you happy. You know this. But I also know the pain you go through every day, and I will not cause you more. Last time was an unintentional trick of the fates. Amor is well within her soul. That is all we can ask for as guardians."

Like a volcano overflowing, magma spews from my pores, and I push at the god before me. "Put. Me. Down," I say evenly but with force behind my words.

He does not want to. His grip holds tight and firm onto my backside, but I push again, and he reluctantly lets go, my body sliding down his, hitting all the delicious ridges along the way. *Gods, how can he look good enough to eat but also make me unbelievably angry at the same time?*

I look up at sparkling eyes and chiselled features towering above me, his wavy hair tumbling around his face. The moon illuminates him from the sky above. My fingers quiver to run through his lush locks, but I hold the urge in. Instead, I clench my fists so I can feel the sting of nails biting into skin as I recentre myself.

Both of us, stubborn in our views, don't relent. Sounds of trickling water run by us, and I look around to find we are by a popular walking path just outside the city proper. Away from the scene of my crime.

Closing my eyes, I take a deep lungful of summer night air and unclench my jaw, looking up at the stars hanging high above us. *Anger won't get me what I want. I need to take another approach.* I step back within his embrace, Janus effortlessly accepting me. My fingers flit across his chest, teasing the exposed skin. A deep rumble comes from within his sternum as I continue my wandering hands movement upwards. "Please, *cor animae meae*, just give me tonight."

I kiss the place over his heart, a shiver coursing through both our bodies. "On your knees." His tone is forceful as he grabs my hands in a tight grip, only releasing me when I begin my descent. Blinking up at him, my mouth twitches. *Gods, I can taste him on my tongue already*. My knees hit the grass beneath us.

In a desperate haze, I plunge my hands into his black leather skirt. What he shows up wearing is always a surprise. Usually, it reflects what we wear within the mortal realm. *I could get used to the no top look and easy access to his cock.*

My hands glide across corded muscles reaching for his velvety hardness, giving it a firm squeeze. "Is this what you want?" I ask as I pull his cock out into the night air.

The god before me grunts as he looks down at me, wide-eyed and firm-mouthed, the tip of his cock leaking pre-cum. I go to lick it, tasting the richness of his soul within his juices. "No," he rumbles, weaving his fingers through my hair and tugging it backwards so I stare up into his eyes. "I want you spread out before me like a fucking feast, screaming my name until you have no breath left in those pathetic mortal lungs." Good thing I no longer rely on silly mortal constructs such as breathing. My pussy clenches at his strained words. "But"—he surprises me as he continues, reading me like a book—"I know your tricks, woman. And I have no desire to see any more pain in your eyes."

My shoulders sag at his words. He releases my body, and I fall backwards. Janus takes a wide step separating us, his hands tucking away his thick length between the folds of his skirt. I land on my hands, hard soil underneath me, and dig my fingernails into the grittiness beneath. Rage pools within my leaking core, now spilling over towards its target.

"I hate you," I spit at his feet, daggers radiating from my eyes as they travel up his body. The swarm of desire and rage propels me to continue, unbothered about the consequences of going head-to-head with a god. "This is all your fault." I stand, pointing a finger at his annoyingly chiselled chest that gleams in the moonlight. "I wish ..." Stomping closer to him, I seethe fire as I stare into his anguished gaze. "I wish you had let me die."

I notice slight creases forming around his eyes at my statement, sorrow pooling. As much as I want to take it back, my anger would never allow it. He needs to feel what I'm feeling. He has to know the depth of my sadness.

"You wish me to leave, Sabine?" His voice is harsh and cold, a chill running down my spine even though the warm air teases my hair into an uncontrollable frizz.

"Yes. Do what you do best, Janus. Fucking leave," I hiss, and before the last word is uttered from my lips, a loud *crack* sounds, a gush of air washing over my body. Blinking my eyes, I find no god standing before me. Just a lone pathway—one I will spend the rest of eternity walking.

Entwined in Eternity

Present Day, 10th June, 2025 AD

I don't know this woman. I don't know this woman. And, of course, she doesn't know me. Confusion is etched in the lines of her face.

A gruff laugh comes from Pluto. I turn to face him, his eyes soulless. *How could I not have noticed that before? He is completely devoid of compassion. Of empathy. How did I think this god would be anything like Janus?* Pluto's sneer shakes me to my core, and the only thing that makes sense is saving Amor's soul from being trapped down here.

Crack.

My ears pop at the loud echo within the vast space as Janus appears before the table. *My* Janus. My heart melts at the sight of him, but he does not look at me, my heart giving way at his utter lack of regard. Instead, his focus is on the other god in the room—the immortal now in control of my fate.

Fury bubbles quickly within my gut, my blood sizzling in my viens at his utter disregard. I want to shout, "Hey, you, do you remember me? The woman you made immortal? The woman you expressed your love to century after century, and the woman who carried your baby and nursed her through life and death?" My wrath is a licking furnace as I grip my hands in tight fists at my sides, watching on.

"Pluto, what are you doing?" He almost sounds exasperated as his jaw sits tight on his handsome face. *Fuck. Even though I want to kick him square in the nuts, he still calls to me, the sound of his voice an aphrodisiac.* My rage eagerly moves southward to my desperate core.

If we weren't in the Underworld and our daughter's soul wasn't on the chopping block, I would ravage him. Pluto and Pina could have front-row tickets if they wanted to. *It has been too long since I've felt his hard body on mine.* A pang shoots through my abdomen.

Janus's eyes squint, keeping a steady gaze on Pluto. The god of the Underworld's once sinister look relaxing at the sight of him. "Well, isn't this an unexpected surprise, uncle."

"I don't find it so unexpected considering you've brought my heart and soul down to this place. If you wanted my attention, you could've just asked me to visit." *Fuck, did he just call me his heart and soul? And he said it so casually, like he was rattling off his chores for the day.*

Transfer souls through the mortal and immortal realms, check.

Save heart and soul, check.

To be honest, I don't know what else he does. He is a pretty simple immortal. Ferrying souls is his main priority. *And maybe me.* My heart flutters wildly at the prospect. I remind it to settle down. *We still have to hold this god accountable for his sins towards us.*

"It's been so long, uncle. I'd almost thought you had forgotten the way to my humble home." A maniacal smile covers Pluto's face, making me cringe. "I didn't realise you cavorted with humans." He says the last part with a scoff, like we are so far beneath him when, in fact, he is the one beneath us. If I could just get close enough to him, maybe I could shove the onyx dagger he gave me into his chest—the one I secretly squirrelled away into the waistband of my skirt. Though I doubt I'd hit a heart.

"You know very well of my interactions with humans, Pluto. Now, why the fuck do you have my human here?" The way he says "*my human*" makes my knees weak. *Get a grip, Sabine.* How, after close to 3,000 years, does this god still make my body swoon with sheer hunger at his words?

"*Your* human? Well, well, well, uncle, do you have feelings for the mice that scamper within the mortal realm?" Fire returns to Pluto's gaze, finally giving away his agitation at this conversation with Janus. However, his face represents a cool statue, devoid of care.

"I could care less about the humans, but she"—Janus points a finger right at me without looking, which is impressive, as he continues his words—"is mine, and I will not be sharing her."

So now *he decides to claim me.* There was a point when he would've torn anyone apart for laying a finger on me, but after Amor, he withdrew, thinking giving me space to love others would heal me, which ultimately led us here.

Fuck, we were so stupid. Maybe I should've just found a nice family each lifetime to dote on like he wanted.

Now, our daughter's soul is here, and it's all my fault. I never expected this, but that's the thing with life—you never get what you expect.

Pluto goes to stand, all eyes on him as he casually wanders over to the human woman. Her eyes become saucer-like when he gets closer. "Since you are here for only the small, unkillable human, you will not be concerned if I ..." His voice trails off, his hands falling at the sides of the woman's perfectly manicured locks.

SNAP.

My heart falls through my chest, and I forget to breathe, her lifeless body falling forward onto the table.

"Out with the fucking trash, I say," Pluto taunts.

My vision goes blurry, air struggling to find my lungs. *Did he just kill her?*

Numbness washes over my body as two warm hands glide over my cheeks—two hands that remind me of the unconsciousness that awaited me in my room when Pluto snapped my neck. Apparently, a signature move of the god.

Running on desperation and fear, my body acts from a place of self-preservation. Ears ringing, I take the onyx dagger from my waistband. Aiming true, I push it forwards into a hard chest.

With hazy vision and warped hearing, my only senses left are touch and taste as familiar, masculine lips meet mine, waking me up. *Janus.* First, my eyesight returns, my eyes flying open to find the comfort of two familiar amber orbs staring back at me, followed by my hearing. Laughing comes from the other side of the room.

Pulling back from Janus, I look down to see the blade impaled in his chest. "No," I murmur. Gripping the dagger, I pull it out to find blood seeping from his chest—the place where his heart would be. "No," I whisper on a sob, Janus's legs giving way underneath him.

I follow him down to the ground, his wide eyes on mine. "Sabine." I hear his gruff voice, but it does not fully register as I try to place my hands against his wound, blood still pouring.

"Cor animae meae." It's a command. His voice shocks me as he finds my ear with his lips. "Do what you do best, my love." Janus pushes the knife in my hands like a silent plea. For the shortest second, my mind doesn't understand his meaning, but then it all clicks.

I'm a killer.

I murder people.

I've signed his death warrant, and if I can kill one god, I can kill two. For our daughter, for Janus, for me. I will have my revenge, and he won't fucking see it coming.

It takes everything within me to rise and leave my heart kneeling on the hard, cold floor, bleeding out. My eyes rim with tears as I hide the god-killing dagger behind my back. "There, you got what you wanted. I stabbed Janus," I shout, not knowing where the abrupt volume comes from, but it soothes the ache in my soul.

Pluto has resumed his seated position at the table watching the proceedings. "Yes, very well done, human. I didn't expect him to go down so easily." Pondering over Janus's body, Pluto's fingers trail through his beard. I inch closer to him.

"What will you do with me now?" I shuffle closer.

"I suppose Pina would like a plaything." He continues his beard-stroking like he has no care in the world. I suppose he does preside over the dead.

"Oh, really? Thank you, Pluto. I promise to take good care of her," Pina exclaims. My gaze drifts to hers—another victim in Pluto's clutches.

His hand moves up to silence Pina, her mouth falling shut instantly. *Poor girl.*

I hear Janus cough behind me, but I do not turn around, everything in me desperate to return to him, to forget about Pluto. But this could be the only chance I get—while my god, my cor animae meae, is bleeding out on the floor.

A fire fills my veins at the thought that the god of the Underworld has taken everything from me. *I will fucking end him with his own dagger.*

Close enough to have a decent shot, and with the god distracted by Janus, I try my luck. *What's the worst he can do? Kill everyone I love? Oh, yeah, he already did that.* A boiling inferno takes over as I fling the blade at Pluto, who's still eyeing *my* Janus.

The dagger finds its mark. I'm thankful for the many years I spent practising my knife skills. "What?" Pluto looks down at his bare chest, seeing the dagger perfectly embedded in his heart.

The coughing behind me suddenly stops, and Pina lurches forward to push the blade further into Pluto's heart, making the immortal poof into a sudden cloud of sulphuric ash, a rancid taste coating my tongue.

My fingers tremble, seeing how he just up and disappeared. Knowing Janus is still behind me I race to him, but he's no longer on the floor. He's standing tall, blood on his white shirt. "How?" I question, moving my hands to his chest.

Janus raises one eyebrow. "How am I still alive?"

"Yes, you idiot. How are you still fucking alive when I struck you with the same dagger?"

His arms move around my body, pulling me close, a smile tantalising me. "You see, a long, long time ago, I gave my heart away to a human woman."

"What does that mean?" I question further. "I already know you love me."

He chuckles, his hand running through my hair. "Well, you see, my cor animae meae, it is not just a figment of speech. My heart is yours. As long as your heart still beats, I will stay alive. You are my lifeline, my salvation, my everything. I gave you everything I am from the moment I let you drink my blood."

"But—" His face is amused at my obvious shock. "But what about Pluto?"

"His heart only belonged to himself, as do all gods'. The only way the god dagger cannot kill is in a situation like ours."

"And what is our situation?"

His fingers grip my chin, making sure my eyes are locked on his. "Our situation, my love, is that we will forever belong to each other. Our souls are entwined as one."

Rapture

Present Day, 10th-11th June, 2025 AD

Pina and I lie on our backs, looking up at the blush-red sky, a soft yellow grass under our bodies. "Is it always that colour?" Everything about this place is categorically different from Earth but also familiar.

Turning around, Pina faces me. "Silly, what other colour would it be?" Not knowing much about the goddess's past, I let it be for now. We have gone through a lot, and I just killed her husband—sure, she helped, but I was definitely the instigator. We don't need to debate on the colour of the sky. It is an interesting change—one I'll most likely have an eternity to get used to.

Once Janus showed me he was healed, I had implored him to go and check on Amor's soul. I hated knowing that was the way her current human body had to end, but I knew Janus would continue to keep an eye on her. If her soul is cycling through the mortal and immortal worlds, I am happy. Death isn't the worst thing that can happen to a human. I am living proof of that.

"Should I give you a tour of the manor now that you're staying?" Pina's big green eyes lock onto mine, expecting an answer.

"Of course I'm staying, Pina. Where else would I go?" I stretch out my hands, showing her my lack of choices. It's either here or back to Earth.

Janus made that clear after our reunion. I may have gotten around Pluto, but I am still not safe. I will have to keep a low profile here in the Underworld. None of the gods can know of my existence. Except for Pina, of course.

If I am found to have god blood, the other gods will send me to Tartarus, an ominous, fiery prison. I thought Pina could stop them from sending me since she technically rules over all parts of the Underworld, including Tartarus, but Janus made it clear that if enough gods were to vote against my existence, she wouldn't be a consideration. I would burn in the fiery pits of hell for eternity.

"What about the mortal planes?" she whispers as if it's some secret.

I laugh. "No way, Pina. The Underworld sounds way more my speed."

She squeals, springing up, pulling me close.

I melt into her, a smile pushing out my cheeks. *I have a friend—one who won't die after eighty years of being alive.*

With Pina the heir to her god husband's lands, she was quick to inform me I was more than welcome to stay. In fact, I was encouraged to. As long as she wasn't a bastard like Pluto, I was happy to call the Underworld home.

Janus and I can spend time here unencumbered by beginnings and endings since the Underworld is a part of the immortal planes. Essentially, when he isn't busy carrying out his duties, he can be here without me having to kill anyone.

For the first time in a long time, I feel like there is a light at the end of the tunnel, even if I am still a secret from the other gods.

Once Pina finishes showing me around her castle—the place is gargantuan—she takes me to a new set of doors that leads off a wide hallway.

"This will be yours and Janus's chambers," she proudly announces as she pushes the heavy doors open to a warm bedroom filled with rich, mahogany furniture and plush velvet couches. It is double the size of the room Pluto held me captive in, with enough space for a mini library, a lounge area and a circular dining table. It is basically a studio apartment.

Turning, I hug my new friend for the second time, tears filling my eyes. I've never had a home for me and Janus before. It's always just been me, but now we have a place for us.

As the sky makes way for inky darkness, I lounge on the feather-down bed. Half drifting off to sleep, I feel the light filled warmth of Janus, his fingers starting to twist my hair.

"You are trouble," smooth words race over my skin as broad hands travel down my body, lifting my nightdress. "Or should I say, you *are* in trouble, my heart." His rough fingers grasp my arse and squeeze tight, making my eyes fly open.

Before he can continue his teasing of my flesh, I maneuvre to sit on the bed, facing him, my gaze quizzical. Janus's perfectly sculpted cheekbones are highlighted by the flickering flames of the fire. Just the sight of him is enough to make me melt. His hand falls to my thigh, testing my resolve.

"I need you to tell me the truth." I place my hands on his naked, broad chest, his eyes heated with lust as he takes in my scantily clad body. "Focus," I reprimand.

A sigh falls heavily from his lips, his hand squeezing my thigh hard. "What do you need to know, Sabine?"

"Why did Pluto want me to kill you?" The question has been playing on my mind. Pluto went from wanting to take my soul to wanting me to kill Janus without explanation. He just expected me to follow his orders, and still, I have no answers. I know nothing about my god beyond the little time we shared on the mortal planes.

"Pluto has been jealous of me for a very long time. He has always despised the fact that I hold Caelus's favour. No doubt, knowing you were alive made him see there was finally a way to get rid of me. He couldn't control you by taking your soul and inhabiting your body, so he decided to control you through our daughter." Janus closes his eyes while he scrubs a broad hand down his face.

"Why couldn't he take my soul?"

His prone body goes still as darkened amber eyes meet mine, his grip getting uncomfortably tight on my leg. "Because your soul belongs to me already, cor animae meae."

My fingertips glide up to the short, dark beard lining his lower face. "What about the onyx dagger?" My breath comes out short as a wicked grin moves over his lips. No doubt he can smell how my body greedily reacts to the sight of him.

"The onyx dagger is forged in the pits of Tartarus. It is the only known artefact that can imprison a god, but it cannot be wielded by one."

"What do you mean 'imprison,' and why can't a god wield it?" The questions come thick and fast.

"The god dagger is just a way to trap a god in Tartarus. You can never kill a god. We are beyond death. And having a human wield the dagger is just a fail-safe. I don't think it's ever successfully been used before, even though some have tried." My eyes must be popping out of my head because

Janus laughs at my expression. "You have done something no one else—not even a god—has done before, Sabine."

I don't think "pride" is the right word, but hearing I was able to do something gods cannot does fill me with a sense of accomplishment that maybe my immortality could mean more one day. At that idea, a thought comes to me. *Can a human be made into a god?*

I squint at Janus, squirming under the pressure of his touch, feeling a certain need to get back to what he was starting earlier. "Why am I in trouble?" I lean into his chest, whispering the words. My heart beats rapidly, giving away my excitement for the god who came for me. *He can finally come for me.* My heart swells at the knowledge, knowing he'll be able to come and go as he pleases from the Underworld—from our new home.

He nips at my lips. "You are in trouble because you summoned Pluto when I told you not to."

His hands travel down to cup my bottom, lifting me up to straddle his front. He stares at me, an infinity moving behind his familiar eyes.

"You gave me no choice," I respond.

With my nightdress fully around my waist, exposing my arse, a loud slap comes down, moving all the way to my pulsing epicentre. I grit my teeth, my pussy clenching in time with the jagged beats of my heart.

This feels more like a reward than a punishment, and by the utterly wicked grin showing on Janus's face, he knows it too.

"There is no excuse for your utter dismissal of what is mine. And now you leave me no choice but to punish you, Sabine." *Smack.* The stinging pain comes again.

I push my bottom back into the air to soothe it, but that does not last long as smack after smack rains down on me, making me fall over his body and his hard cock, groaning at the feel of him. *Gods, my god is too good to be true.*

"Is this what you wanted, me pliant to your will, my god?"

Grabbing my arse cheeks tight in his hold, he murmurs in my ear, "All I ever want is you needy and pliant underneath me, screaming my name so the other gods can hear everything they'll never have." My stomach flutters and my pussy screams to be filled at his words.

"How about we get to the screaming part, then, because I'm fucking starved for you, cor animae meae."

I do not have to tell my god twice as he pulls his cock out to find its home.

The First Time

The Past, 552 BC

I didn't expect this death. Travelling through the thicker parts of the forest usually keeps me well hidden from any travellers. Only people who don't want to be found travel this deep. I found him half-dead with fever, propped up against a tree. He probably picked up some disease from contaminated food or liquid. You have to be alert within the forests; they will swallow you up and spit you out if you don't have a keen eye. Fortunately for me, I do not have to worry about trivial things like human illness. The god blood comes in handy for something.

I am keeping my distance from Janus. I thought that if I came out into unknown lands, kept my distance from the humans, I wouldn't have to face him, but day by day, the need to see him grows. Every time he's shown himself through either my making or the divine fates, I breathe a sigh of relief, knowing I'm not crazy.

Taking a lungful of damp leaves and filtered sunlight, I crouch down before the slight man and take his pulse. Loose, barely there beats come through clammy skin. *I should just put him out of his misery, but then I will see him.* A shuddering breath comes from the skin-and-bone man resting at the foot of the tree. My own heart squeezes at the sight, still not able to fully comprehend death in all its forms. I've helped injured or sickly people pass before, but that was with their permission. This man is so far gone I doubt he will ever awaken.

"Damn it." I pull my silver dagger from my boot and hold it at his throat. Slicing deep and quick, I pull the blade across skin and watch as the man barely moves, his blood trickling down his chest.

Prone and stuck in time, I await the inevitable.

A *crack* blasts through the surrounding trees, and my neck prickles with the feel of *him* behind me. My mind desperately wants me to turn around and seek my god out.

"Run." The growl he gives reverberates through my body, settling heavy at my core, igniting me with passion.

Confused, I stand and turn to face Janus, the only god who holds any true meaning to me. The god who has stolen my heart day after day over the last two centuries. "What?" I look up at the imposing man before me. Every time I see him, it's like no time has passed at all, his ageless features a balm to my weary existence.

He takes a step forwards, his eyes raking my body. "I"—another step—"said"—another step—"run." His face angles down towards mine, his dark hair falling in front of his eyes.

"Why?" my voice breathlessly leaves my lungs. My body is a magnet for him, this god created from every fantasy my soul can conjure.

A chuckle moves through him. "Because I've been patient for 200 years, Sabine, and I can't wait any longer to feel your body writhe in pleasure against mine."

Taking a heady gulp, I move backwards, bumping into the feet of the dead man. "What if I want that too?"

Standing straight, he takes a deep breath through his nose, closing his eyes, smelling me. Smelling the pool of need for him making its way down my leg.

He shakes his head slowly. "Sabine, you do not want me. You do not want what I will make of you. I will ruin you. This all-consuming need I have for you will destroy both of us." His eyes are black as he penetrates my soul. "Now, I will not tell you again. Run," he barks at me.

On instinct, my body trips backwards, and I manage to stop myself from falling, instead turning on my heel and disappearing into the forest.

Legs and arms pumping furiously, I run from Janus. *Why am I running?* I almost stop, my heart beating out of my chest, fire burning up my throat. Excitement soars through my veins. But something tells me to keep going, keep pushing. That the adrenaline pumping inside my body is enjoyable.

I know I could never outrun a god. *Surely, he has tricks I can't even fathom. Plus, the man is a giant. He'll be on me bef*—

"Oooofff," the air rushes out of my lungs, a wall of muscle running into me from behind.

Warm air tickles my neck as Janus inhales my scent for the second time. "Fucking delicious, and all mine," he rumbles.

"Wh-what will you do with me?" My words come out shaky like I don't already know he's here to pillage my body for his own pleasure. *Gods, do I want that?* I'm a slut for him and only him.

"Have you let them touch you?" he scoffs. He means the other humans. I've almost been tempted at times. My human body still feels pain and pleasure the same way any other human without immortal blood in their veins does.

"No," I whisper. I wouldn't allow anyone else to touch me. Not since the last time. Since those men almost tore me apart. Janus saved me. He went against his laws and gave me his blood to keep me alive. My life, my body; it all belongs to him, including my heart.

"Good because this"—he grasps my hips and brings my body flush with his every muscle—"is mine." He explores with his hands, skimming across my stomach, making butterflies swarm at the gentle touch. "You've forfeited yourself to me. I own you." My whole body shivers at his admission, and if his hands weren't on me, I would crumble to my knees.

Turning in his grasp, I latch onto smouldering eyes. "I want you, Janus. I want everything you have to give me, even if it is only us making love in this forest."

His eyes burn into mine, his forehead coming down to meet me as his strong hands hold firmly onto my jaw. "This time, Sabine, we will not make love."

"No?" I tremble, my breath coming out short and sharp, my core continuing to leak for him.

"No." He smirks. "This time, I'm going to fuck you until you can no longer walk straight."

"Okay," I answer quickly, giving him my full consent even though my body is giving him all the permission it needs. I grasp onto his toga and grip him close to me.

"Okay," he growls and latches onto my lips. Squeaking at the unexpected fullness of him, I sink into his arms. Janus easily lifts me up to wrap my legs around his torso. With my hands free to wander, I place them in his hair, teasing and pulling as we fight our tongues into each other's mouths.

Pulling away from our kiss, Janus brings us over to a tree and orders me to hold onto one of the upper branches. When he undoes my grip around his waist and hauls my pussy up to his face, I hold on tight. Pushing past my skirts,

I hear him growling his frustration at my layers until he finds me bare underneath.

"Fucking heaven," I hear him grunt, his tongue going to taste my core, making me buck uncontrollably in his arms. My hands clench harder around the branch above, feeling small pieces of bark embed themselves into my fingers. Janus's arms push down on my thighs as he latches onto me, taking broad sweeping licks with his tongue, teasing my clit. My orgasm builds quickly, his mouth lapping at my pussy.

"Oh my god, Janus, I'm going to—" His tongue stretches through my core and pushes in deep. "Oh, god. Oh, god. Oh, god," I moan louder and louder. He continues to punish my body, my god giving me continuous pleasure, not requiring air.

Just as my muscles start to lock up and my eyes go splotchy, his full lips find their way to my clit, and I'm done. Releasing the tree branch above me, I scream as my need flows out of me.

Leaning over his head, Janus changes our position and places me on my hands and knees, facing the leafy ground below.

Soon, his hands are pulling me from behind and turning my face to meet his. Greedy lips find mine as I taste my sweetness, coating him. He growls loudly. Janus grinds himself needily against my arse, my own body pushing back, basking in the friction.

Pulling away from the kiss, dark, lust-filled eyes find mine. "The only god you will ever scream for is me."

"Yes," I whimper. Broad hands lift my skirts, finding my core dripping.

"You're so wet for me, cor animae meae." His finger finds my opening and pushes on a soft spot inside, the ecstasy making my back arch. My pussy pools around him. I close my eyes, my body falling forward, hands digging into the soil below.

"Only for you," I whisper breathlessly.

"If you let anyone else touch you, I will end them." His declaration is one I can happily get behind.

"Only you, only you, only you," my voice rises as he takes his thumb and rubs it in punishing circles over my clit.

"That's right. You're mine." He pulls his finger out, and I hear clothes rustling. I groan, my body expectantly waiting for him. "Look at me, Sabine." Eyes flicking effortlessly to his, I smile wistfully. "This"—he pushes his hard cock against my entrance—"is mine." And he pushes all the way in, pain and pleasure mixing together at his sheer size, each thrust inward hitting new, undiscovered parts of me. Opening my soul to his.

"Yours, my cor animae meae."

Our lips find each other again as we are a tangle of limbs, moving desperately to feel the utter rapture we sense in each other's bodies.

Another orgasm finds me, Janus moves in a punishing rhythm, my body bending to his will. Our groans of pleasure mix, my body shattering under his. His own orgasm is not far behind as I feel him fill my aching core. *Finally, he's mine.*

Destruction

Present Day, 10th August, 2025 AD

*N**ot long now.* Sending souls through the gateway is an endless activity. A never-ending brutality that has become second nature over the millenia. I don't even blink an eye. The humans don't see me—except for her, and she only sees me because I let her all those centuries ago. I showed myself when I pulled the souls from those savages' bodies. I stood back and watched for a moment, but once I found her two pools of endless galaxies staring back at me, a rage welled within, a silence descending. I'd never known such fury before until I finally acknowledged it boiling within. The way the humans treat each other is barbaric. It is their way. It never mattered to me before.

Not until her.

Seeing those green-blue spheres with gold flecks roll back into her perfectly sculpted face, bruised and battered, tore at my very fabric. Her wild, flowing auburn hair, clothes ripped and shredded as those bastards thrusted into her ... I snapped. It was barely a thought. It was in-stinctual. They dropped like flies.

When I'd sought her, crumbled underneath the soldiers' lifeless forms, it was the first time I felt a heart come to life within my chest. *Star-crossed.* It didn't seem possible, but I felt it within my being, within my soul. She was the only thing that mattered to me, and I could never be without her. We were forever doomed to walk separate paths, and I still gave her my blood because I was an egotistical god who didn't care for consequences. Saying no to her was my hardest challenge in life. The fates were having a field day with me, surely. If I could seek counsel with them, I would curse them out.

With my job set to autopilot within my sphere, I travel back to her, my cor animae meae. My soul's heart.

I feel her in our new favourite spot—the hot springs beneath the manor. Since Pluto's untimely departure, I've spent more and more time here in the Underworld with Sabine. Just the thought of Pluto sets a bad taste in my mouth. Dread fills me to bursting, knowing I nearly lost her to him. He was a jealous bastard who wanted to bring me down in the eyes of Caelus, my father. Unfortunately for Pluto, I am the god's favourite. *I should have known I needed to protect Sabine*—the thought eats at me. I've never warred with my own mind so much in my life, but when it comes to her, I can't help myself. She is always the first and last thing I think about. Every second of the day.

Having her fall into Pluto's hands that night was purely coincidental. I could never leave her. I would never. I was all talk. I knew she would kill again and again, finding me. The expectation was there, and I wasn't about to break it. Until I was held up with Caelus, God of the Sky. That's the only reason I missed her. I'd left Pluto in charge of taking souls through the doors. I just never expected he would find her, show himself to her. It was rare he ever needed to step in for me, but Caelus had to brief me on the latest council ruling: tailored god pairings. Forced marriages between unmarried gods to produce offspring.

I'd scoffed at the new decree. Caelus knew my job was one of the most taxing of all of the gods. It required too much movement. I would never be paired. My heart, body and soul were already owned.

"Fancy meeting you here," a uniquely smoky, feminine voice greets me from behind, a hand trailing down my clothed back. Just her touch through clothing sends tremors down to the tips of my toes. The only time I've ever felt mortal is within her arms. She gives me everything I didn't know I needed.

An infectious, pink-lipped smile greets me as she pushes up to grasp the soft cotton of my shirt, landing a kiss on my chin. *Give me strength.* The whisper is a plea to the fates. My cock already stands at full attention just from that one touch.

"What are you wearing?" My eyes gaze over the barely there black lace one-piece she has on. Compulsorily, my hands move to grasp her hips, the warmth of her skin grounding me to this moment and drowning out the chatter in my head. Souls move in and out, but Sabine is the only being who has ever taken my full attention.

Her long lashes flutter. "Do you like it?" She whispers seductively.

Hip popping, she poses temptingly for me. "I don't care what you are wearing, cor animae meae. You are the most exquisite thing in all existence."

Pouting lips turn up as she moves to throw her arms around my neck. I haul her up my body. "Good, because I fucking hate underwear. Even pretty lingerie. This thing is giving me a serious wedgie." She chuckles into my neck, and I rumble along with her, the only sound in my head her sweet symphony. *Fucking bliss.*

With some godly magic, I help her out and release us of our clothes. Her body sighs. "That better, mea amour?"

"So much better." Wiggling up my body, her soft skin slides against mine, hinting at all the ways I want to have her, especially the feeling of her wrapped around my cock, her sweet whimpers and desperate screams when I inevitably give in to her.

"Since you're a dirty girl, I think it's time I bathe you," I almost purr as I stroke her soft, naked skin.

"I'm barely dirty," she protests until my hands inch their way under her thighs, teasing the soft curls there.

A soft squeak comes from her lips, making me want to suck all the air out of her precious lungs. Obsession doesn't even come close to how I feel about this woman. I want her tangled within my limbs, joined at my hip, stuck on my cock. Fuck, the impracticality of it. But I will just have to settle for our hearts beating as one because there is always one thing I am sure of: this woman stole my heart, and I never want her to give it back.

Gripping a fist in her thick hair, I yank her head backwards to expose the delicate skin of her neck. Sweet, spring florals fill my nose. I suck down every aroma of her enticing body. My lips skim her quivering veins as I nibble towards her chin. "You have blood all over you, and I need to wash it off."

"What? I don't—" Sabine starts to say until she puts two and two together, my sharp canines piercing her most delicate skin. A whimper leaves her lips at the initial sharp sting, but as soon as I begin to suck, she falls completely at my mercy.

Blood is a delicacy among the gods. Usually, they steal humans for the sole purpose of bleeding them, but I would never bleed Sabine beyond a taste, though she is utterly delectable. It is the closest substance the gods have to a drug since they do not need human sustenance to survive. When we take blood, it's a connection to the person's life force, to their heart and emotions. It's toxic to sense such primitive feelings in my form. The only rule we have about drinking blood is never to share our blood with the humans.

I broke that rule, and I continue to break it as I tear my bloody mouth away from the delicious neck before me. Tension and euphoria fill my veins, my cock needing her syrupy heat.

Glazed eyes find mine. I grasp my wrist between my lips and dig deep, ripping the skin open, quickly pushing it towards her mouth before it closes over. She can usually get two decent draws before it completely heals. The deeper I go, the longer it lasts for her.

As soon as Sabine's lips suction around my bite mark, we both shudder. I didn't even feel the breaking of my skin, but her lips on my body sets my senses to spark. Her fingernails dig into my arm, she pulls on my wrist, taking in a deep draw, my immortality bonding her to my side for eternity, forever burning in each other's rapture.

We only started sharing blood after we came to the Underworld—a novelty I had not indulged in within the mortal planes due to the simple fact that I knew it would make me even more crazed for her. And the gods would have had a higher chance of detecting her if she held more of my blood in her system.

Now that she is in the Underworld permanently, she will be harder to detect since this place is filled with immortal beings of all stages of power.

When I feel the wound close, I pick my human up and sling her over my back. She barely utters a word, high on the feeling of my blood. Walking us to the nearest hot spring, I sit on the carved seat in the sizzling water and bring her body down to straddle my lap, her pussy bumping against my cock.

"Are you just going to tease me?" she whines, her peaked nipples rub along my chest, her tongue licking my collarbone.

"No, I'm going to devour you," my words muffle when I pull her lips to mine, the soft glow of the sconces lighting the cavernous space, illuminating the twinkle in her eyes. Our mouths tumble in rhapsody, my sunshine mixing effortlessly with her springtime. Over the years, she has sometimes veered towards the mellow coolness of winter, but her true nature has always been life—my life.

Sabine groans into my mouth as we tie our bodies together, her wet skin sliding up and down against my torso. "Who's the tease now?" I moan into her mouth.

She laughs breathily as I grasp her rocking hips. "Seems only fair considering I've been waiting all day for you to come home. I think your blood is making me even crazier for you. If that is possible." Wedging our bodies together she pushes her wet core up and down my rock-hard cock, set to explode before I even enter her. "What are you doing to me?" She keeps her pace, shuddering above me, my cock still very much aching for relief. A deep moan leaves her mouth. "Finally."

"I think"—I pull her slackened body up, digging my fingers in tight—"you—" We lock eyes, her head tilting.

"Me?" she rasps, gripping my shoulders.

"Yes, you"—I line up my cock underneath her—"are doing this to me." I slam her down, thrusting up, making her head fly back as she screams. I close my eyes, savouring the way she pulls my cock deep within her tight heat, every inch of her trying to draw me into her. "You stole my godsdamn heart. You're a fucking witch, and you don't even know it."

Soft lips find mine, giving a sweet kiss before turning savage and biting down. "And I'm never giving it back," she sneers wickedly at me. I begin to pump into her from below, savouring her fight.

"I wouldn't have it any other way," I murmur, my lips finding hers again.

"Good," she groans, lifting her hips up slowly and slamming them down, building us both to orgasm. My cock barely makes it out alive as her walls pulsate around me.

My hot warmth fills her, and I pull her body impossibly closer. "You're mine."

"No, you're mine," she sighs, her fingers finding my own, locking them together.

"Cor animae meae." The groan is guttural. We both know it's true. She fucking owns me. *A human, owning a god. My father would have a field day if he knew about her, about us. We will just have to live in sin forever.*

I have no problem with that, but I need to make sure the spitfire riding my cock understands her safety is paramount to me. Though, with the amount of blood I've shared with her since she's lived in the Underworld, I'm surprised she hasn't gained the essence of my power within her yet.

"I want to go with you tomorrow." Her voice is honey-saccharine but sure.

"Sabine," I groan, knowing she's trying to get me to concede with her at a weak moment. We've had this conversation every day since she's been in the Underworld. With her taking more and more of my blood, maybe, someday in the future, us travelling together will be a possibility. But it's still too early.

Placing my hands on either side of her face, I make her look at me, her head tilting up. "I now understand what the humans mean when they say someone is giving them a heart attack."

Her teeth go to nip at my face like a cute shark. My eyebrow raises. "I am more than a heart attack, Janus, God of Beginnings and Endings."

Moving her hips up oh, so slowly, I feel every part of her pussy grip onto my still hard length inside her. "What else are you, then, cor—"

Once she reaches the top of my cock, her eyes twinkle mischievously back at me. "I'm your destruction."

The beginning and the ending.

More Stories

by R.A. Raine

Want more Sabine and Janus?

Visit R.A. Raine's website (www.raraineauthor.com) and
sign up to her newsletter for the bonus epilogue!

Why Choose Romantasy

Sing Me Awake

Book 1 in the Bonded to the Gods trilogy

Sing Me Free

Book 2 in the Bonded to the Gods trilogy

Acknowledgements

This was a story I've always wanted to write, yet Janus and Sabine didn't make themselves fully known to me until the start of this year (2025). I hope you enjoyed reading their story as much as I enjoyed writing it, and I hope you found some comradery in Sabine. I know she's a bit unhinged, but that's her charm.

Burn couldn't have been possible without the help of some amazing women who helped me make this story really shine.

To my beta readers Clara, Kaehla, Clare, Paige, Samantha, Jeannie and El. Your help was invaluable. Thank you so much for reading the beginnings of this story and your continued support. It means the world to me.

To my all around beautiful and amazing editor, Brittany. Thanks to your care, this story is everything I wanted it to be. You are a rock star.

And lastly, I want to thank all of the amazing readers in my life who continue to support me and tell me they are excited to read the next book!

About R.A. Raine

R.A. Raine is an author from coastal Australia. When she's not immersed in epic romance stories, you can find her searching for fairy portals, spending time with friends and family, or reading tarot cards.

She loves to write about inner turmoil and love, so that is what you will find in her stories, with tension and spice thrown in for good measure.

If you would like to connect with R.A. Raine you can find her hanging out in her Facebook reader's group or on Instagram and Tik Tok @r.a.raineauthor.

Enquiries can be emailed to Rebecca at raraineauthor@gmail.com.

9 781763 802452